ITALIAN
for
Christmas

NICOLE SHARP

The WRITING Moose

For more information visit: www.nicolesharpwrites.com

To the city of Florence, who captured my heart
and continues to inspire my dreams...

ITALIAN
for
Christmas

— 66 —

I'M ALWAYS GOING TO REMEMBER
HOW FLORENCE TASTES LIKE YOU.
LIKE COFFEE AND PASTRIES AND A
COOL HUMID FEBRUARY MORNING.
- FROM *THE ITALIAN HOLIDAY*,
NICOLE SHARP

— 99 —

Chapter 1

"So, you have le informazioni per la Casa Villa." The stylish, brown-haired woman – whose name tag read 'Angela' – beamed a smile as she finished a laundry list of instructions for staying in the rented farmhouse called the Casa Villa.

Angela glanced around the room and snapped her fingers as she recalled what she'd forgotten to mention. "Finally; to use the stove, just remember to turn gas off at night. And when you create the fire, open la ..." She frowned then crossed the space to the fireplace and pulled a lever up and down. "Up when you make the fire, okay?"

Isabelle nodded as she was handed the keys to the five-bedroom Italian farmhouse her parents rented so the entire family could vacation together over the Christmas holiday.

"And you will move to Italia soon, sì?" Angela asked.

"You must have talked to my dad." It wasn't so much a question as it was a statement made by the child of an extrovert who was very proud of his children. She continued, "I'll be in Rome for work, but only for a year."

"Ah, but you will love Roma." Angela picked up her purse from a nearby chair and slung it on her shoulder. "So, soon, the snow will be finished in Chicago and la tua famiglia can take the flight to join you."

"I hope so." Isabelle gave a terse grin.

Angela pursed her lips and shrugged, as if to say, 'it happens.' She squeezed Isabelle's arm. "You have my number, telefono. If you have problems or needs, per favore, phone me." Another sparkling smile flashed as she zipped up her long coat, gave Isabelle one more nod then swept herself out the right side of the large double wooden door, calling,

"Ciao, buonanotte e Buon Natale! "

Isabelle walked back down the long foyer into the large open concept living room, dining room and kitchen and made a slow circle around the space. Angela said she'd turned the heat on, but it was still cold; the large space would probably take quite some time to heat. She glanced at the fireplace, that was probably the solution. But it'd been a while since she used one.

As she traced her hand across the light wood surface that topped the island across from the stove, she looked over the upgraded space admiring the exposed light wood beams, modern silver appliances, neutral beige sofas and two dark green patterned armchairs.

"An Italian farmhouse for Christmas," her voice echoed. "Or is it a villa?"

It had been a fabulous idea when her parents brought it up last year. The whole family together. Isabelle; her two brothers, along with their wives and kids; her parents and her dad's sister (Isabelle's favorite aunt); and her grandmother (Dad's mom) had all enthusiastically planned this once in a lifetime retreat.

Insert the irony of a severe storm system that had currently grounded her entire family, all who lived just east of Chicago.

Except for Isabelle, who'd been working in Los Angeles the past two months. She'd already sent her belongings to the Eternal City. And since there was no snow in LA, she seamlessly winged it to Florence, Italy.

She sat down heavily at the large rectangular table that could easily seat eighteen. It was covered with a sage green tablecloth, and in the center a wreath of olive leaves, eucalyptus, dried oranges and burlap bows hugged a trio of stocky white candles.

In front of that display was a group of welcome gifts: a yellow packaged cake, a cellophane bag of what looked like chestnuts, and a bottle of wine and olive oil, both with labels reflecting the name of the vineyard where this farmhouse rested. In front of the offerings was a decorated postcard that read 'Buon Natale.'

She pulled out her phone and checked the time, a little after six p.m. She dialed her oldest brother, Ethan, the one who'd taken charge of getting a group of fifteen from Chicago to Florence.

"Izzy!" he answered out of breath.

"Hey. I'm here. At the farmhouse ... villa." She tried to sound enthusiastic.

But she was disappointed. And tired. And she hadn't seen her family in months. She'd been so excited when she got off the plane, almost skipping into the arrival area where her family was supposed to be waiting for her; as her plane arrived thirty minutes after theirs.

Only, all she found were a handful of texts to call Ethan.

Then there was a fiasco of misunderstandings at the car rental place. She was supposed to take one of the three vans that had been reserved; but for a reason she didn't understand, the man at the desk shrugged and insisted they were "no longer available."

Frustrated, she decided to leave that mess for later and walked with her two large suitcases, one stuffed with presents for her nieces and nephews, to get a taxi; only to be told by the driver that while he could get her to the small Tuscan villa (which was thirty minutes outside of Florence), it was going to be quite difficult to get someone to pick her up. She asked about Uber or Lyft, but the driver blinked at her question. Obviously offended.

So she hefted herself and her luggage back to the car rental desk to rent a car. Of course, it was the holiday season. Which — as it had been explained — caused a run on rentals. And since the airport in Florence wasn't international, and surprisingly small in nature, her options were limited. At least that's what she gathered from the bored rental agent who begrudgingly clicked around on a computer until slipping a set of paperwork and keys on the desk, signifying the 'finding' of a car and the end of their interaction.

The slight hike to find the vehicle ended with her snorting in disbelief as she stood in front of a red Smart Car – with its two seats, an engine and just enough room in the trunk to put a slip of paper. She held her breath as she opened the 'trunk,' then let it out when it seemed her two bags would *just* fit inside.

Of course, when she climbed in and saw it was a manual, a burst of laughter escaped. It had been years, but she could do this. She typed the destination into her phone's GPS, then gave herself a big pep talk: "Izzy, if you can test fragmentary remains, you can definitely drive the world's smallest car in another country."

As she pulled out of the sparse rental car lot, she ground her teeth and hissed, "c'mon" as she passed three large vans; though she wasn't given too much time to think about it as she merged out of the airport and into early evening traffic.

The cars around her came to life with an unnerving aggressiveness; even the scooters pushed in on either side. A few stalwart trucks kissed her bumper and most of the revving beasts surrounding her continued to honk and yell.

She swore under her breath, gripped the steering wheel tighter and tried not to imagine what an accident in this aluminum can of a car would be like.

Eventually she lost the traffic as her wind-up toy car exerted itself, climbing up curving roads into the Tuscan countryside. Driving in Italy should have been a delightful dream, but the reality was an intense ordeal. She was racing the last dusty rays of light through winding roads that lacked streetlights; and despite GPS, didn't have any real idea where she was.

Thankfully, she made it in time.

The farmhouse was surrounded by scattered old homes, all of which had been converted into rentals. The whole estate looked like a small village, completely surrounded by orchards and grape vines. There were tasting rooms attached to the buildings where the wine and olive oil were made.

As Isabelle drove past the collection of eight separate buildings, down a cypress-lined dirt road, she came to her destination: the Casa Villa. A three-story, peachy orange house, with closed, dark green shutters and surrounded by trees and foliage. There was a gravel parking area in front where Angela had been waiting for Isabelle.

And now, finally sitting alone in the large, chilly, echoing house in the middle of nowhere, there was an eeriness that made the place exude less *Christmas Vacation* vibes and more *The Shining*.

Her brother interrupted her tired reflection, "Is it gorgeous? The pictures online make it look pretty amazing."

"It's gorgeous," she admitted. "They even gave us a free bottle of wine and olive oil." Wine she was going to crack open the second she was off the phone and pair with the cake thing. She hadn't stopped at a store, thinking there might be something close by, but the only 'convenience' was a closed 'bar' fifteen minutes back down the hill.

"This is a mess." He sighed. "At this point, if this storm passes, the airline said they *should* be able to get us on flights by Monday."

Three days from now.

It wasn't like the storm was the fault of her family, but she was frustrated with the situation.

She forced a positive attitude. "Well, that's still in time for Christmas and the New Year."

"You should go explore Florence. You need to learn the language anyway. Don't wait for us. Just ... have fun."

Have fun. The instructions brought tears to her eyes, she didn't want to have fun alone. She wanted her family with her, and she wanted the air around her to be filled with the vibrations of ridiculous arguments and the smells of cooking and laughter and the planning of who was going where and when and how.

She wiped at her eyes with the back of her hand; this was just exhaustion and the unexpectedness of the situation. She'd shake it off after a good nights sleep. Her family would be here before she knew it.

"Izzy?"

She cleared her throat and touched the bag of nuts. "Do you know how to roast chestnuts?"

"In a pan?" Ethan's smartass reply helped center her.

"Part of the welcome gift is a cake and some chestnuts." She took a deep breath. "Okay. This situation is what it is. Three days isn't that long. Keep me informed, but right now, I'm going to go get drunk then go to bed."

"Everything will look better tomorrow," he offered.

She blew out a sigh, but agreed, "Yes, everything will look better tomorrow."

Chapter 2

"Le sta bene?!"

So, things weren't necessarily looking better.

"I'm sorry," Isabelle offered to the man standing next to her car as she rolled the window down. He was looking at her concerned and at the same time, slightly shocked and confused.

"Americana?" he said as he crouched down so he was at eye level with her.

She'd woken with a headache: wine induced. Hungry: the cake hadn't curbed her hunger. Cold: she needed to figure out how to use the heater. And in desperate need of caffeination: coffee would fix that. So she climbed back in the Smart Car: destination – grocery store. She'd have coffee, cook herself breakfast, shower, and maybe *then* head back into Florence to explore.

She tossed her phone, passport and wallet into a small crossbody purse and made her way thirty minutes back to Florence. When the GPS promised the next right would take her to the grocery store; she turned only to slam on the brakes because of an accident on the opposite side of the small street. She stared for a moment, human nature dictating such things, when she noticed a well-dressed man with dark hair and shining brown eyes walking away from the group of bystanders trying to help. He waved to the cars on the other side of the street and her; an attempt to direct traffic.

Only Isabelle was so taken aback by him – the way he wore the hell out of his dark gray suit, the black shirt, the purple tie, his well-kept short hair, slight stubble, and downright shocking Italian handsomeness – that she mouthed 'oh my' to herself just as he made eye contact and winked at her.

Well, *that* little moment shocked her so damn much, she overcorrected the turn she was making, causing the right tires onto the sidewalk. When she tried to correct *that* issue, she slammed on the gas, brake and clutch, like she was just learning how to use them, and finally came to a full stop when she hit a sign post.

Luckily, the small car and her lack of any real speed was stopped by the pole the sign was attached to.

"Signorina?" he asked again.

"I'm fine." She knew she was turning red. "I'm just ... not used to the streets. And I didn't know ..." she cleared her throat, unable to gather back the last few lame words as they tumbled out, "... how much room I had."

He tilted his head and raised an eyebrow. "This is a very small car."

She opened her mouth to defend herself – she could say this was her first time driving in a foreign country or that she was hung over or that she wasn't used to a manual... *or*, just admit that his wink caught her so off guard because she hadn't been winked at like that or even *looked* at like that in so long; and the damn little gesture was lovely and needed and she'd ride that high for at least two weeks. In the end she just reiterated, "It's a very small car."

"Are you okay?" he asked, his accent alluring.

"I haven't had my coffee yet." Now, *that,* she was happy to admit.

She put the car in park and turned off the engine, deciding it was a good idea to check out the damage.

The man stood and held out his hand in offering. She took it, trying not to notice how warm it was or, when she was closer to his six foot frame, how he smelled as good as he looked. And she was definitely *not* trying to stealthily dip her head toward her armpit to make sure she didn't smell too awful.

She dropped his hand and rolled her eyes as they stood next to each other and studied where the bumper was nosing the post.

"I think everything is fine," he said.

"Me too." She gazed across the street at the real accident. The drivers of the cars were laughing and waving their hands about. "Are they okay?"

He nodded. "They are fine. I saw the accident and thought perhaps I would help with traffic. But then you appeared and I forgot my original task."

The comment drew her gaze to his; and he winked once more.

She gave a soft laugh and instead of dismissing his comment and gesture, admitted, "I like your suit."

He smoothed the lapels. "Do you?"

"So what should I do?" She glanced around. The few cars trying to get past on either side had emptied the street, leaving only the group gathered on the other side and Isabelle's car.

"You need coffee." He shrugged. "So I'll take you."

"Oh, no. That's okay."

He pointed across the street. "There is a café just there. We can have an espresso and you will tell me about yourself and I will try to get you to agree to have dinner with me tonight."

I mean ...

But coffee *did* sound good. And it really *was* needed.

She glanced once more across the street. The red neon sign did say café. And it looked darling; there were tables outside separated from the sidewalk by a hip height partition of frosted glass and heat lamps.

"I really do need coffee," she admitted. "Is your car somewhere?"

"Down the street. I was visiting a friend."

She glanced around once more. "Okay."

He held out his hand in introduction. "I'm Matteo. Matteo Arcuri."

"Isabelle Miller." She took it, once more captivated by its strong warmth.

He double downed on his allure and called her "Isabella." Adding the 'a' to the end of her name, the sound of it all slowly twirling with a sexy Italian lilt – she definitely wanted people to say her name this way for the rest of her life.

She dropped his hand as if she'd been electrocuted and nodded to her car. "Matteo, don't kidnap me or anything, but could you drive and find parking?"

He gave a slight bow of his upper body and she made her way to the passenger side. Before she climbed in, though, she gazed at him over the roof of the car, shaking her head while under her breath, laughingly drawing out the words *'Oh ... my'* once more.

Chapter 3

Inside, the café was raucous with morning visitors standing around the bar where a barista was deftly churning out picture-perfect cappuccinos and espressos. There were only three tables inside, so Matteo suggested they sit on the patio near one of the heat lamps.

Isabelle took an appreciative sip of cappuccino and sat back in her chair. She still needed some sort of pain killer for her headache, but she hadn't tossed those in her purse; hopefully the caffeine would eventually work.

"So, Matteo ..."

"Isabella," he returned and a little flutter under her ribs whispered that they would truly appreciate it if she'd ask him to repeat that; only this time maybe he could move slightly closer, narrow his gaze and deepen his voice even more.

"Do you live in Florence?" The dull question had a bit more of a forced edge to it than she would have liked, but she *was* trying to quiet her internal dialogue.

"No, but my family lives outside of Firenze. I am visiting for the holiday season. And I have work here as well."

"I don't mean to keep you from anything if you're going to be late ..."

"When a lovely woman is visiting Italy and in need of coffee, it is a man's job to accompany her." The quick pulse of a slight eyebrow raise accompanied his words.

Isabelle hid her smile behind the rim of her cup, admitting, "You're pretty smooth," before taking another drink.

He sat forward and corrected, "I'm intrigued."

"You watched a woman crash into a pole because she was distracted by something ... rather ... handsome," she responded, which arranged a lovely smile on his face and might have added a dimple on his right cheek, but his trimmed stubble kept it secret.

"See, intriguing," was his reply.

Besides her questionable driving skills, she wasn't sure how intriguing exhaustion could look. Isabelle fought an urge to reach up and make sure her auburn hair had stayed in the bun she'd put it in as she tried not to worry whether her face was splotchy from the long trip, overindulgent evening and exhaustion.

"So, Isabella," he began and she physically had to stifle a shiver, which she now chalked up to lack of food, "are you visiting for the holiday?"

"Yes, my family and I came for the holiday, we're staying through the New Year." *Eventually,* she silently added.

He angled his head and sadly stated, "Ah. So you are married."

"What? No ... I mean ... I was." As she stammered to explain her current life situation, the question if *he* was married snapped her attention, so she glanced at his left hand. No ring. No tan line. "What was I saying?"

"You were married?"

"I *was* married. I'm not anymore. We were young and stupid and not right for each other. We parted ways amicably."

"Ah, but is there someone special? Who is also on holiday with you and your family ...?" he led.

"Just *my* immediate family. I'm single. I mean, I'm alone." She spit the words out and felt she'd twisted the moment so much, why not continue. "I'm not seeing anyone at the moment. How about you? Are you married? Or have a significant other?"

"I am single." He lowered his voice with that simple declaration.

Isabelle took a deep breath, raised her arms above her head, which made her sit up straight, then dropped them in a swift motion and blew out a breath. "Matteo," she began again, "I got in late last night. I drank way too much wine. I have a headache that isn't going away. I need more coffee and I am starving."

He stood, pointing to her cup. "Finish that. I will take care of the rest and return shortly."

She hoped he didn't think her physical reset was strange, but she'd probably never see him again; so for the duration of her time with him, she'd rather take in the handsome Italian man with a full stomach and a relieved headache.

He returned with two aspirin and a tray holding a glass of water; two pastries; a roll with tomato, basil and a glorious thick slice of mozzarella; and another cappuccino.

She groaned as he placed it in front of her. "Okay, now *I'm* impressed."

As he settled himself once more Isabelle asked, "What do you do for work? Where are you from originally? Why aren't you seeing anyone and what's one thing I shouldn't miss this time of year in Florence?" She picked up the sandwich but before she bit into it added, "And how old are you?" Then — hoping she still appeared ladylike — she appreciatively and voraciously ate the sandwich.

He picked up one of the pastries, took a small bite and after returning it to a plate rubbed his hands together to rid them of crumbs. "Allora, you should walk the city center in the evening, when the light show is projected on the side of the buildings in Piazza della Signoria. And also wander through the Christmas Market in the piazza near Santa Croce. I have had a few relationships, but they never strengthened as time went on, just weakened. I have not found a woman that intrigues me in a very long time." He let the beguiling accented words whirl around for a moment and land properly between them before continuing, "I am thirty-four years of age. I grew up near here, my parents, two brothers, sister and many nipoti still live nearby. However, I live in Roma now, and work for un'agenzia di intelligence."

Roma, you say?

A new flutter erupted at the news of his living circumstances. She was grateful she was chewing, allowing her a moment to decide how much she was going to share with him. He was a stranger. He'd also distracted her enough to get her in an accident. (She scoffed at the idea; *some accident, Izzy.*) But he did right by buying her coffee and a few decadent pastries. Still, she decided to hold onto the ace in her pocket that she was moving to Rome.

He turned the questions around. "Where are you from? What do you do for work? How old are you? Why aren't *you* seeing anyone, and can I take you out this evening?"

"I'm from Chicago. Thirty-two. I'm currently working for a university and I think ..." she cleared her throat in an attempt to find a little courage, "going out with you would be fun."

"It would be," he pointed to himself, "I'm a fun guy." Then he nodded his head in her direction. "Should I point out that you did not answer the question about a relationship?"

Isabelle took a drink of her cappuccino in reply and he waved his hand gently through the air. "Okay, forse, it was not a very gentleman question to ask."

"For say?" She asked after the Italian word he used instead of indicating if he was right or wrong about his assumption.

"It means perhaps."

"Forse," she repeated happily.

He adjusted his tie. "This evening, we will go to dinner and then, forse, we will walk the streets of Firenze and see the lights."

"Forse." She shrugged and took another bite.

Matteo's phone rang and he frowned. "I am sorry, but I must ..." he glanced at the number, "work." She waved him away with the pastry she was holding and he took the call. He stared off into the distance behind her, his smile never fading as he talked animatedly with his free hand. After a round of "ciao, ciao, ciaos" he hung up. "I apologize."

"You said you were working while you're here?"

"We are searching for a pickpocket," he explained. "A man who fits the description was brought into the stazione di polizia, but it is the wrong man."

"That must be some pickpocket." Isabelle sat back, her stomach full and head soothed from finally being medicated, caffeinated, and watered.

"Possibly ..." was the way Matteo excused any further discussion about his work.

"You said you work for intelligence? Like the CIA?"

He shook his head, "it is more of a law enforcement job."

"Is that why your English is so good?"

"It is good, isn't it?" He laughed.

"Okay Matteo, since I've already interrupted your day enough—"

"No, this has been an unexpected delight, una distrazione divertente."

His voice lowered, wrapping around the Italian words.

Surprising emotions in her chest flitted about as if she'd just been compared to Cleopatra. But as far as she knew, he could have said she was ridiculous and a pain in the ass.

Not knowing how to answer him, she cleared her throat and asked, "Where and when should I meet you tonight?"

"I can pick you up."

She thought about the curvy Italian roads that led to the villa. She could drive, but because she was in Florence, she'd probably have a glass of wine and then she'd have to wait to sober up and then she'd have to drive the haunted winter roads in the dark.

When she didn't answer, he offered, "Or I can meet you in the city center if that would make you more comfortable."

Isabelle only briefly hesitated, remembering the aggressive driving she'd experienced the previous evening.

"I'm staying at ..." she started, pulling her phone out of her purse to get the name of the property, "a wine estate. It's called Torre a Cona in Bagno a Ripoli. It says it's Florence still, but it's almost thirty minutes to get there and I just met you, but I wasn't anticipating having to drive. It's not that I can't drive ..." *Isabelle,* she demanded, *pull yourself together.* She turned the map toward him. "Is it too far?"

He held her hand in his as he studied the map and muttered, "I'm about to be smooth again."

"Are you?"

He winked and caressingly offered, "I would go further just to have one more glimpse into your soft green eyes."

She nodded as the butterflies that had been trapped in her chest released into her bloodstream, leaving her voice barely a whisper, "Yeah, that's pretty good."

Chapter 4

Isabelle stood in front of the mirror in the room she'd designated as hers, lips pulled in a tight line as she studied herself. She was still freezing from the cold shower she was forced to take; because if there was a water heater, it had walked far away from this property. Pair that with the lack of working heater to bring the internal villa temperature up rather than down ... well, she was freezing. And since she only had thirty minutes left before the agreed upon time when Matteo would arrive, the choice to start a fire didn't seem like a viable option.

She tilted her head, at least the cold water had done wonders for her pores. She ran a hand through her hair, thankful the slight wave was cooperating tonight. After applying the last touch of lipstick she gave a nod to her choice of 'date night' clothing: dark jeans; a teal sweater she thought complimented her auburn hair; long silver earrings; and stylish, yet sensible walking shoes. She hadn't come prepared for a date in Florence. She'd packed 'family outing' clothing. Good for meandering the streets all day, holding kids and possibly hiking up and down the stairs of bell towers. *Not* clothes for dating a man who wore a suit like ... well, she grunted and told her reflection, "the way you imagine an Italian man would wear a suit."

She gave her reflection one more confidence boosting nod before heading to the front door.

While they'd agreed on a time and she'd given him the name of the property, she had a nagging apprehension he might not find it in the dusky light. And since they hadn't exchanged numbers, if he didn't show up, she'd never know if he got lost or just changed his mind.

Maybe it would be better if he stood her up.

"Stop it," she chided, opening the front door to watch for him. And was exhilarated and relieved (and nervous) to find a small, four-door gray car pulling to a stop right on time.

Isabelle gave a half wave, and when he climbed out, the vibration in her chest let loose once more in reaction to the man; to what he was wearing and *how* he was wearing it. She gave a soft laugh and muttered to herself, "*Come on ...*"

The front porch light beamed the perfect ember glow to accompany Matteo's arrival. He wore dark jeans; a black, high-neck sweater; a camel colored overcoat; and a sexy, lopsided smirk. The sweater was tight enough for her to make out slight muscle definition and she wavered between closing the front door — then yelling through it that she was sick and couldn't go out tonight — or just grabbing the lapels of the open jacket to pull him close enough for her to see if he tasted as good as he looked.

It didn't help that when he approached, the first whiff of his enticing aftershave caused her legs to wobble. But she wasn't allowed any time to implement defenses against her latent insecurities because he stepped past her personal space and said, "Isabella, you are a vision," just before gently touching his hands to the side of her elbows and leaning in to brush a kiss on her cheeks.

When he stepped away, she wanted to pull him back and insist they never leave this moment.

Matteo's eyes shone bright as he continued his compliments, "You smell good too."

Isabelle cleared her throat and stammered, "Too ... you ... do ..." She licked her lips and reformed her sentiment. "Matteo, you smell and look good too."

"Grazie." He looked around her, his eyes searching the entrance. "We have time, if you'd like to introduce me to your family ...?"

She turned around, following his gaze, as if she were about to produce fifteen snowed-in people out of thin air. "Actually," she turned back and narrowed her gaze, "you're trustworthy right? I mean, you're definitely a flirt, but you're not ... evil." She shrugged at the word. "Right?"

He pulled out his wallet and handed over a business card. "If you need a reference, you can always call my supervisor."

Isabelle took the card and read it, then held it up and defended, "In this day and age, a girl can't be too careful."

"I agree."

"Good." She took the card and put it in her purse. "Because my family's not here. *Yet*," she emphasized. "They're snowed in and their flights have been canceled so they haven't been able to get out of Chicago."

"Ah, well, I am sorry for the troubles, but maybe a little happy too." His lips parted in another disarming smile. "Because maybe this is the reason you agreed to a date with me tonight, sì?"

"It might have had a little something to do with it."

"Then it is destino you crashed into me, so you won't be alone during Natale."

"I *bumped*," Isabelle held up a finger to make her point, "into a pole."

He beamed. "And I'm lucky you did. So, Isabella, are you ready to see the city center decorated just for you?"

"You know, you keep this up and you're going to either make me think all Italian men are like you or you're going to make them all pale in comparison."

Matteo reached for her hand and brushed a warm, soft kiss on the back of it, then glanced up through lowered lashes and whispered, "They will all pale in comparison to me."

As Matteo drove into the city, Isabelle was reassured by the way cars and scooters seemed just as angry with him and his vehicle as they'd been with her. And she was further comforted by the choice of allowing him to drive as they got closer to downtown and the designated pavement markings for traffic flow became mere suggestion and the number of cars grew exponentially at each stoplight, as if Matteo's car was metal and he had some homing device turned on to attract more vehicles.

"Centro, the city center, is the heart of Firenze, the original city. Like all other cities, population helped it grow," he explained, "but centro is where we'll see the cathedrals and museums and popular shops."

"And you can't drive in the area, right?"

"Sì, only taxis, a few buses and delivery trucks are allowed in specific areas at certain times of the day."

"Oh! Is there a bus that goes from the villa to the city center?" she asked, out of curiosity for herself and her family if they ever arrived. Because the reality of trying to figure out where to park three large vans among the crowded sidewalks they drove past suddenly seemed daunting.

Matteo gave a playful reprimanding tisk. "I can pick you up."

"All sixteen of us?"

"Certo," he shrugged, "of course."

She studied his profile, lit blue by the dashboard. "Okay, but just to make sure I understand you. Before my family gets here, let's say I want to go to the store for butter; you'll drive *all* the way out to the villa for a round trip that is completely out of your way?"

He waved the idea away. "No, of course not. I would *bring* you the butter and we'd go for a walk through the olive trees and have a tasting of the wine, then you'd offer me a coffee in front of the fire."

"I see."

Visions of … whatever the word for sexy Italian sugarplums was … well those were suddenly given flight and danced in her head.

Matteo let a few beats pass before he flashed a grin and softly requested, "Please, need butter soon."

"Well if you really want to help me, there might be something you could do."

"Is there?"

"Yeah," she tried to sound seductive, "because of you, I had to take a cold shower tonight."

He raised his eyebrows as his smile grew.

She reached out and drew a circle on the back of his hand gripping the steering wheel. "I have no idea how to turn on the water heater in that place, and I haven't been able to figure out how the heat works, and it's been a while since I used a real fireplace with a flue …"

He nodded but his attention was on her hand as it dropped back into her lap. When they came to a stop sign, he took advantage of the moment to make eye contact. "So you need someone to heat you up?"

I mean, he wasn't wrong.

Matteo took turn after turn, insisting they were getting closer to the restaurant; but the way the streets were shrinking as the buildings encroached more into the road, she wasn't sure they would have any driveable street left in a few more blocks. She'd begun to hold her breath and suck in her stomach muscles while pulling on the car's door handle, as if she could help it shrink as they passed cars barreling toward them on the opposite side of the road.

Matteo didn't even flinch.

"Is the traffic in Rome like this?"

"Sometimes. Sometimes it can be a little worse. There are more people there."

What could be 'a little worse' than this? she wondered.

Finally, he pulled into a driveway and stopped in front of a green wrought iron gate, the back of his car left sticking into traffic. He threw on the brake and hazard lights, climbed out to enter a number in the wall-mounted keypad, and then he was back, pulling through the opening gate into the parking lot of an apartment building.

"A friend offered the use of his apartment's parking, " Matteo explained. "He is in Calabria until the new year." He threw the parking brake on, then was out of the car like a shot.

Isabelle thought maybe there was an unspoken hurry and tried to follow his example, but quickly realized what he was doing when he reached her door.

As he held out his hand, she was about to quip a smartass comment on how smooth his actions were, but when her hand fell into his strong, warm grip, the words were sucked back in on a slight breath.

He gave her enough of a tug that it propelled her closer to him than she'd anticipated, his smile indicating it was right where he wanted her. She placed her free hand on his chest to steady herself (she reasoned), and cocked her head. The bright lights of the area shining down on his head should have given him an unseemly look, and it did flush out a few slight wrinkles, but ... Isabelle sighed, "A person can't look this good."

"I was just thinking the same thing," he returned as his head lowered slightly, his lips parted; almost imperceptible, but Isabelle caught the motion and was *very* interested in what that slight move meant.

There were matching subtle smiles of anticipation and shared shallowness of breath when Matteo slammed his body into hers and the bottom of his chin thudded against her forehead with a grunt.

"Minchia," he grumbled at the same time Isabelle muttered, "What the hell?"

A bark from behind Matteo pulled their attention. A large dog was pawing at Matteo's leg, jumping forward and backward as if trying to get him to play with him.

A few steps away was a voice calling to the dog.

Matteo grabbed the dog by the collar, crouched down and soothed, "Eh, cucciolo. Che fai?"

Isabelle gave the dog a pat, as much as she wanted to disapprove of the animal's excited antics that interrupted a *very* promising moment. But he was cute and gave her a new insight into Matteo. She wasn't sure what 'cucciolo' meant, but she would bet money it was sweet.

"O, Matteo!" The voice that called to the dog now called out a greeting.

"Ciao, Piero." Matteo stood and shook the offered hand of the man who appeared out of the shadows.

"Piero, this is Isabella. Isabella, Piero, the cousin of the friend who let us park here. But Piero and I went to Università together also."

Piero stuck out his hand for Isabelle but when she took it he stepped closer and brushed the common kiss greeting on her cheeks.

"Nice to meet you." She smiled, patting the dog who was nosing the side of her leg.

Matteo snapped his fingers to get the dog's attention, and gave him a pat on the head when he backed away from Isabelle. "Be nice to my friend."

Matteo and Piero exchanged pleasantries for a moment. Isabelle understood the word ristorante, and thought she caught the unspoken eye of Matteo as if he were telling his friend, 'you and your dog have awful timing.' To which the friend laughingly slapped Matteo on the back and seemed to reply, 'it is what it is and I'm amused.'

Goodbyes given, Matteo gestured back to the main gate that housed a pedestrian entrance. "Shall we?"

Chapter 5

I sabelle slipped her purse over her head and zipped up her jacket as they walked. The setting sun had taken any slight warmth with it; and the buildup to that interrupted kiss, that had heated all parts of her, had also cooled.

But her disappointment was replaced by the beauty of the scene opening up before them.

"We're almost there," Matteo reassured, "where we are going for dinner."

"It's fine." She held her arms out, palms up, as if that would physically offer the street scene they were walking as tangible proof. "I'm in Florence."

This first real, feet on the ground, nighttime sight had her enamored. And it wasn't just one thing that captivated her, it was everything. From the cobblestones beneath her feet to the arched doorways on either side of her; the variations of earth tone brick buildings broken up with smooth plastered buildings where the windows flaunted shutters of green or brown, and a few others had wrought iron décor.

"God," Isabelle whispered, so as not to interrupt the early evening magic, "this is gorgeous." It was postcard-perfect and they were only on 'some street' close to a restaurant.

And to top off the enchantment, swags of white lights were strewn between the buildings, back and forth, skating above the street in long strides.

If Isabelle had a vision of what Christmas might look like in Italy, this exceeded expectations.

In the same way the traffic accumulated the closer they got to the city, people began to multiply when they turned onto another street. All were bundled in long coats, some wore beanies and gloves, and most had scarves.

The same lights were strung above, leading the way, while the glow from storefronts they passed spilled onto the cobblestone road, adding a charm that made Isabelle's head bobble as she tried to take everything in; but all too soon they arrived at their destination.

"Here we are." Matteo reached to open the door. It was a wide glass door with a metal handle framed by a gray stone arch draped with lighted garland. On either side of the door existed ornate scrollwork, and wrought iron light fixtures added to the glowing entrance. The name etched into the door was the only indication that this was a restaurant.

A young man in dark pants, white shirt and a black tie greeted them, "Buonasera."

Immediately, the smells of onion, garlic and other baked goodness encompassed them. The soft din of conversation, ting of silverware against dishes, and flickering candles on each table along with dim overhead lighting, exuded an air of romance and invited lingering.

The walls were exposed brick in all shades of red; and pillars throughout the dining area – where arched ceilings intersected – created cozy nooks for diners. Sconces with subdued lighting hung at various intervals along with black and white photos of Florence.

They were shown to one of the cozy nooks that gave the illusion of isolation. Isabelle shrugged out of her jacket and thanked the maitre d' who held her chair.

"This is stunning," she whispered as she sat forward and gazed around to take in her surroundings. Only, when she settled back and focused on Matteo and his smile in the soft light, she was grateful she was sitting down; his friendly intensity did some fascinating shiver work up and down her spine.

"It is *molto* bella," he returned.

Isabelle decided if she were ever asked to list what a person should do in their life at least once, she would definitely add: At some point, one should have the opportunity to sit across from someone who looks at them with such interest, it causes time to stand still.

And while time stood still Isabelle drank a romantic glass of red wine;

had crostini that melted in her mouth; tortellini in broth that she would probably search the rest of her life to find again; a side of baked onion in a parmesan sauce that was enlightening; and finally, a grilled beef filet that made her question if she even knew what good cooking was.

The entire meal was eaten slowly, reverently; while the wine loosened their bones and increased lowered lashes and suggestive smiles.

Matteo and Isabelle shared stories about childhoods and school. They talked about Christmases past; how they both longed for home the older they grew, but in a nostalgic way. The truth of the bygone days seemed that their childhood households were often chaotic interactions with siblings and they both were filled with the youthful hurriedness to break free from the chains of their parents and make their own way.

"I was so excited to see my family and I don't know if they'll make it." Isabelle rolled the glass between her hands.

"If they don't show up, I am inviting you to be with me and my family. You can experience a traditional Italian Christmas."

"What is a traditional Italian Christmas?"

"Allora ..." he churned the air in front of him with his hand as he thought of how to explain it, "it is all about spending time together; there is a lot of importance placed on family, but there is also a lot of importance placed on the food."

"Well, if it's anything compared to this meal, that's not such a bad thing." She grinned. "If my family doesn't show up and it isn't an imposition, I'd love to join you."

"Perfetto." He slipped his glass to the center of the cleared table. "Now, if you would permit me. I'd love to take you for un digestivo."

"A digestive?" she asked.

"An after-dinner drink. But first we could have a little walk, see more of the city on the way."

They left the warmth of the restaurant, but with the wine coursing through her veins, Isabelle wasn't too cold. Matteo gestured in the direction they were to go, and offered his arm for her to link her elbow through.

"I can't remember ..." She retraced her past boyfriends and ex-husband; other than her father on her wedding day as he walked her down the aisle, no one had ever offered her an arm. "Thank you."

"Prego, my pleasure."

The streets they meandered were cobblestoned and lit by strands of stars, twinkling at various intervals. Isabelle continued to be enchanted; every brick, door knocker, inset of bronze nameplate, and each worn wooden double door blended together into eyefuls of glorious architectural design that was so Florentine and Italian it didn't seem real.

She thought about pulling out her phone and opening her location to find out exactly where she was in this historic city, but she left it to rest in the front pocket of her purse, rather enjoying the mystery and surprise of it all.

Matteo caught her attention with a smile and raised eyebrows. She copied the gesture, until he turned his attention to a place just ahead of them, slightly hidden, peeking out from behind the buildings they were walking next to. With a jut of his chin he indicated where she should look.

And she looked.

And her feet slowed to a stop.

Because just beyond the twinkle lighting, reaching into the cold December night, was the gleaming dome of Florence's famous cathedral, so very close.

Isabelle's mouth opened in wonder, but she couldn't find the words and felt this was what her brother meant when he told her to go see the sights.

"Andiamo." Matteo squeezed her arm and she happily followed because the Italian Renaissance was waiting to dazzle her.

Chapter 6

T he enormous Christmas tree that glowed from liberally draped lights on each branch, was dwarfed by the jewel of the Renaissance, the Duomo. Her imposing, abundant beauty was well lit and even though there were more people and noise in the surrounding piazza, when Isabelle craned her neck to take in the very top of the structure and the matching bell tower standing beside the Grand Dame, they all disappeared from view.

"You see pictures of it ..." She shook her head. "I looked up some things about Florence over the past few weeks, and of course pictures of the Duomo are all over the place, but until you're standing in front of it ..." she trailed off in awe. The only descriptive words she had were repetitious. Still, there was something about adding her voice to the millions that had come before her and would come after, so she whispered, "She's amazing."

"She?" Matteo asked.

Isabelle turned to him and found the same intense, respectful, yet heat-building study Matteo had been making of her all night.

She soaked in the attention for a moment before reaching out to touch the air in front of her, as if by extension, she could touch the marble walls of the structure. "It has to be a she, something this detailed and glorious ..." she trailed off.

"*She,* is spectacular," Matteo agreed.

That loose feeling in her chest, the flutter, the temptation that was Matteo, made her confident which 'she' he was referring to.

"There's more to see, if you're ready," he offered.

"Yeah," Isabelle sighed, giving the Duomo one last once over, "show me everything." Because if the streets left an impression and the Duomo took her breath away, what else did Florence have to offer?

They walked down another street, this one wider, a thoroughfare. Lights and warm drafts from store doorways spilled out onto the gray brick road, enticing the passerby to enter. The eye candy in each storefront created the need for one to do a sort of shuffle walk and flick their head from side to side, so nothing was missed. All of the colors and scents encompassing Isabelle, added to the intoxication of the evening.

Windows were simply made up with appealing allure, but there was an aloofness to it as well; as if the stores in their Italianness were saying, 'we don't really need your patronage, but maybe you want to look.'

There were purses, perfumes, clothing and tourist trinkets. Cafés selling gelato, one in particular with a fountain of chocolate spilling down the length of an entire wall, filling the air with chocolate seduction.

The wander down the street was over too quickly, but as it gave way to another piazza revealing even more Renaissance architectural royalty, Isabelle didn't care.

There were a lot more people here than had been in front of the Duomo; probably because of the projection of lights creating a show of color against the buildings.

"This is the Piazza della Signoria." Matteo brushed the information against her ear. She wanted to ask him to say that again, it was so appetizing. And somehow he got the hint, because after a few more steps, his mouth was against her ear once more. "A few years ago, Firenze began this light show, projecting images on several buildings throughout the city." He nodded for her to walk across the large piazza.

A red brick, steeple topped building, loomed over the square; she recognized it from the quick searches she'd done online. It was called the Old Palace, but she hadn't delved into any other history; that was something she was supposed to do with her family in tow. Although, this man she currently had in tow was quite the unexpected stand-in, and so far, Isabelle had to admit he was doing a damn fine job.

A statue of Michelangelo's *David* stood guard in front of the steps of the Old Palace. Isabelle pointed. "That's not the real one, right?"

"A reproduction," he verified.

She followed his lead to the left side of the Old Palace, where a fountain stood. A stark white marble Neptune kept watch from atop the center of the fountain, overseeing a group of mythical creatures, sea monsters, and bronze river gods.

"People didn't like the fountain at first," Matteo said.

"When was it sculpted?"

"In the fifteen hundreds. It was supposed to be a glorious thing, but the people were not impressed. Actually, do you see the plaque on the side of the building, just there?" He pointed out a white marble rectangle set into the brick of the Palace, about hip height from the muscular Neptune. "The people did not revere this fountain as a piece of art, they actually did laundry and washed out their ... what is the word ... the holders of their ink."

"Inkwells?" Isabelle offered.

He nodded. "I think so, yes. Well, that plaque says if anyone is caught doing such things, they would be fined."

"Really? That's so cool." It was such a lovely little detail, one she probably wouldn't find in any guidebooks. "What year was that?"

Matteo stopped their progression, moved to investigate the marble warning closer, then after a moment he pointed. "Ah, 1720."

"Then I suppose we will have to find somewhere else to clean our inkwells." She gave a slight shiver.

"Are you cold?"

"No," she lied as another shiver caught her, then admitted, "maybe a little."

He walked her around the back of the fountain and turned so they could see the whole piazza with an unobstructed view of the projected lights, then said, "I'll be right back."

She nodded as he backed away from her and when she thought he was going to turn, he stopped. She widened her eyes in silent question, then, without any pomp or circumstance, he crossed the distance between them, cupped her face in his hands and settled his lips on hers.

Her eyes fluttered closed as she leaned into him and parted her lips with a sigh; he tasted of the cool humid air, red wine and heat. She wasn't sure if the rushing sounds were coming from the fountain or the blood pumping through her veins.

He pulled away too soon, though his fingers had wound themselves lightly through her hair. "I'll be right back," he reiterated, though he didn't move. Instead, he let his gaze study her face before brushing one more kiss on her lips, before finally taking his leave.

She watched the confident man swagger away and let the phrase that had come to mind when she first laid eyes on him breathe out, *"Oh ... my."*

He made his way to the opposite corner from where they'd entered, to a glowing stall with printed cashmere scarves hanging in decoration around the entirety of it.

Isabelle grinned, not just enchanted by the forethought of Matteo, but by the whole evening. The whole day actually. She wondered what she'd do alone, had planned on using her guidebooks to see the sights and maybe even bring out her language book to practice, since she *was* going to be here for the rest of the year. Her things were already in storage somewhere in Rome but she didn't have to be there until the fifth of January.

However, unexpectedly meeting a local who helped her with the sightseeing and immersing herself in the culture, was truly a pleasant surprise.

When Matteo arrived at the stand and began to touch the different scarves, she wondered what he'd pick out for her. Though she'd have to wait a while to see as the stand was crowded with customers.

Her attention was interrupted by a family with four kids, all talking animatedly, pointing at the lights and asking questions; pulling the parents' attention in a myriad of directions.

Isabelle smiled, made space for them and watched as the youngest took his teddy bear and, for reasons only known to the small child, threw the treasured toy at the fountain. Isabelle watched wide-eyed as it perched itself on the edge. His parents, who were barking orders while zipping coats and answering demands of the older children hadn't noticed what had happened. Though, the little boy, realizing his mistake, began to sob. Not loudly, but with a wobbly lower lip and watery eyes.

"Oh, oh it's okay," Isabelle soothed.

She glanced around her, and even though there was a slight gate meant to keep people out, what harm would it be if she quickly, stealthily, stepped over the gate, grabbed the child's precious bear, and returned it.

What harm?

That's one of those questions, Isabelle thought, that litters the side of the paved road to Hell.

The *harm* was instantaneous comical mayhem.

The kind that seems to last forever as it happens, slowly, with wide eyes; but in reality, takes the briefest of moments.

The second Isabelle put her knee on the edge of the fountain to grab at the bear, it took a backward dive into the water, its black button eyes sparkling as the damned beast somehow pulled her into the fountain with it.

All at once, the attention that hadn't been on her at all, was blatantly in her face.

Arms reached for her as she sputtered and found her footing. She was confused and shocked, not only by what had happened, but also by the cold water and now cold air that wrung her out; all of which was accompanied by people yelling at her in a language she didn't know.

Two officers with white leather sashes and matching belts with strapped guns, were pulling at her hands and arms to get her out. Her hair was a matted mess in her eyes and as she was tugged over the edge and back onto dry land, she had just enough of a view to focus on an even more menacing presence on the other side of the gate – this one wore a bulletproof vest and held an automatic weapon pressed against his chest.

"I didn't mean to," she chattered, then realized, by some miracle, she was holding onto the stuffed animal. "I was trying to help."

As she was escorted past the family, who were (rightfully) pulling their children away from the scene and looking on with ridicule, she held up the bear as high as she could (which wasn't much since the only thing she was allowed to move was her wrist). But she waved the bear at the family as she declared once more, "I was just trying to get the bear."

She dropped the animal, which drew a screaming cry from its owner and his parents, whose initial ridicule turned to confusion.

"I didn't steal it! He threw it!" she insisted as she was escorted from the fountain, away from the crowd, away from the piazza, and toward a waiting police car.

"Wait! I'm on a date ..." Her teeth chattered and as the officers spoke sharply at her, all she understood was the word 'illegale.'

She wasn't 'arrested' in the usual sense – no restraints were put on her wrists – but her purse was liberated from where it hung in a drenched mess around her body then she was pushed into the back of the car. One of the officers who initially pulled her out of the fountain climbed in the driver's seat, switched on the lights, and waited for the pedestrian traffic around them to clear.

Isabelle turned all the way around and gazed out the back window, looking for a glimpse of Matteo. How the hell was she going to explain this?

Then she saw him. Arriving back where he'd left her. Only now, there were people talking all at once to the other officer who was taking statements. Matteo must have overheard what they were saying, because his vision darted toward the back of the car. Isabelle waved both her hands dramatically to create movement so he would see her.

And she had to laugh as he inclined his head, confused, a frown creasing his forehead, but an entertained smile pursing his lips.

She shrugged in apology as the car pulled away, and was curious (and grateful) as she watched him get the attention of the officer taking statements. *What would that conversation be like?*

Isabelle settled against the back of the seat and finally wiped the wet hair out of her face and felt a little better.

Because while she didn't know everything about Matteo, she had a feeling he'd come for her. He seemed like he was the kind of man who was good in an emergency, partially due to his job, but also his easy going laid-backness probably made him good at smoothing feathers as well.

Isabelle nodded and muttered to herself, "He can handle a tourist accidentally falling into a five-hundred-year-old fountain."

Chapter 7

The police station was close by in a five-story building with pale yellow stucco and green shutters, surrounded by a gated perimeter.

After watching her purse being handed over to a tired woman sitting at the front desk, she was escorted through a maze of offices and high-ceiling hallways. The few people who were working the late hour all seemed to come out and stand in doorways to chuckle or shake their heads at her; apparently it was a quiet, uneventful evening and her antics were all the rage. She was brought to a room where eight desks were scrunched at awkward angles. The officer leading her, crossed to the farthest desk and pointed to the chair beside it, suggesting (through hand gestures) that she take her jacket off and sit down.

She cringed as she hung her dripping coat on the back of the chair and sat down with a shiver. The officer frowned and muttered something before he left her alone in the room.

Eventually he returned holding a towel, and a stiff, yet very warm and very dry blanket he draped around her shoulders. Then, after he put the towel on the floor under her dripping jacket, he left again.

For quite a while.

For long enough that her body heat stopped her shivering and her wet clothes were now just damp and uncomfortable; which led her wandering mind to wonder where the water in the fountain came from. Was it fresh or recycled? Was it gray water with swimming microorganisms she should be concerned about? She dipped her head down and took an experimental sniff. She just smelled mildewy. So hopefully it wasn't that bad.

An hour passed (according to the clock on the wall of the room) and finally the officer returned, this time with a small ceramic cup and saucer. "Questo caffè è per te," he said and handed over the steaming cup of espresso.

Isabelle's forehead scrunched with the ridiculousness (and at the same time, the expectedness) of the gesture, but she tried to smooth it out as she said "grazie" and accepted the offering. She took a sip of the warm, bitter liquid and bit back a laugh; even in an Italian police station the espresso was amazing.

Again the man left, but as she watched him open the door at the other end of the room, she thought she heard a laugh that she'd heard several times over the course of the evening.

Whether it was wishful thinking or he was actually nearby, remained to be seen. Either way, she hadn't been 'talked to' yet. She hadn't been accused of anything and as far as she could tell, no one was in a hurry to deal with her situation. Which left Matteo time enough to help her.

With little else to do, she slouched in the chair and enjoyed the espresso.

Another twenty minutes and this time, when the door opened, a wave of relief eased every muscle in her body as Matteo grinned at her from across the room then followed the officer who'd been seeing to her since her arrival.

"Isabella." The way he said her name seemed to be a question of whether she was okay, while also carrying the weight of 'What the hell happened? I was only gone for five minutes.'

So she rushed out her tired defense, "I was trying to help."

"Are you okay?" He lowered his voice and crouched next to her chair.

While she was touched by his concern, she realized she hadn't truly been worried. Confused and frustrated, certainly; cold, definitely. But never worried.

"I knew you'd come help me."

"You did?"

"I hoped," she amended.

He squeezed her hand. "But you're really okay?"

"I just wish I had some dry clothes."

He stood. "Then we should go."

She rose and glanced at the bored-looking officer who'd accompanied Matteo. "Just like that? We can go?"

"You just need to sign some papers."

"Am I being charged? Or fined?"

"Well, you will have to do two hours of community service before you leave town."

"Really?" She took her jacket, wadded it up and held it away from her body. Matteo shrugged out of his camel knit coat and traded her. She opened her mouth to argue, but he'd already turned his attention to the officer, who crossed the room and proceeded to look through several waste baskets; then finding an empty one, he pulled the liner out and brought it to Matteo to put the wet jacket in.

So Isabelle took the moment to snuggle into his coat, letting the scent – a quintessence of warmth and charm; possibly a cozy fire and deep red wine with an undercurrent of spice – fill her nose. "Mmmm, good coat."

The trio walked out the door, into the hallway and back to the front desk where a new clerk was now working. A document was presented to Isabelle with a pen.

She picked it up, studied it for a moment while chewing her lip, then turned her attention to Matteo. "I'm on a work visa. And I don't know how it's going to look if I show up and already have a record in Italy."

"I understand," he said.

"No, I'm starting a new job with the American Academy in Rome in the new year."

"I know."

"Matteo—"

"You will not have a record," he interrupted.

Isabelle touched the paper while shaking her head. "I'm not this person, who gets arrested. I'm a forensic anthropologist. I've actually worked with a lot of law enforcement over the years," she added, in the hope it would be understood by the two officers standing nearby and help her 'accidental' defense.

"Sì, I know." His eyes were intent, waiting for her worry to leave so she could focus on him. When she was steadied he nodded. "I had a friend do a background search on you." He spoke quickly to the desk clerk who pulled out a plastic box that held Matteo's keys, wallet, phone, and

Isabelle's purse.

"I went through your purse," he said, handing it over, "but only to view your identification."

Isabelle accepted her purse and thought the fake leather might have actually saved the things inside. "I was getting around to telling you about my job," she muttered.

"That you are una antropologa forense?"

"It sounds good when you say it." She pulled out her phone; the battery life was at five percent, but it still worked.

She took a deep breath and met Matteo's patient gaze. "I was going to tell you that I'm moving to Rome for a year. For work."

"You don't *have* to tell me anything."

"I thought ..." She blew out a breath. "When you told me you were from Rome this morning, I almost told you, but it seemed weird because we'd just met and if you were a creep or ... a weirdo, I didn't want you to know I was gonna be in Rome. But we were having such a nice night, I was going to tell you when we got to the bar. But that was before I dove into the fountain."

"It is a nice bar." He grinned.

"I bet."

"Ah, it's been there for fifty years, it will be there a few more nights. We will try again later." He leaned toward her so he could whisper in her ear, "I was having a *very* nice time tonight as well."

The officer waiting for them took offense with the intimate action and gruffly called "Eh," holding his palms up and following with an Italian diatribe that Matteo answered; the exchange eventually ending with a hand held up by Matteo along with the request, "Un minuto." He turned his attention to Isabelle and pointed at the form. "Isabella, this says you agree to do the community service and if you do not show up for it, then you will be charged a fee of three thousand five hundred euros."

"Three thousand five hundred euros?!"

"You are lucky they are not kicking you out of Firenze, the people take damaging their city quite seriously."

"You can get kicked out of Florence?" The worry she hadn't felt since she had been hauled out of the fountain finally showed up.

"Sì, there are many tourists who have been deported, fined and had criminal charges levied against them."

That's all she needed; for her family to finally arrive after she'd been banned from going back to the city center.

"Matteo, this little boy threw his stuffed animal at the fountain and began to cry and his parents weren't paying attention and it was just perched there, and I thought I could help and get it, but I never thought I'd fall *in* and I *never* meant any disrespect."

Matteo touched her arm to calm her, then pulled out his phone and after scrolling, slid the paper over, took a photo of it, and handed the phone to Isabelle. It took a moment for her eyes to focus, but he'd opened a translation app for her.

She took a deep breath and began to read through the document, it was exactly as he'd said. She needed to do two hours of community service before the thirty-first of December this year, then all charges would be dropped and no fine charged. The event would be overseen by Sig. Arcuri.

"Overseen by you?" she asked.

"I asked a few favors."

"So there's no secret agenda." She read through it once more.

"No," he said, with enough levity in his voice she believed him. She had to believe someone.

She clicked the pen and signed her name as she muttered, "Where do I do the community service?"

The frustrated officer who'd been waiting for her to sign, turned the paper toward him, slammed it with a stamp, said something to Matteo then waved them both away.

"What?"

"He would like us to leave." Matteo didn't seem put out at all by the evening or the attitudes of other officers as he nodded toward the door that would take them out to the hallway and finally back onto the streets of Florence.

Isabelle shivered as the cool night air swept over her, but was glad her hair was dry. Matteo turned her toward him, pulled up the collar of his coat she now wore and began to button it. His last action was to reach into one of the pockets and pull out a folded cashmere scarf, teal green with dark paisley flowers. He opened it then proceeded to drape it around her neck. "Before we were interrupted," he teased.

She lightly touched the fabric. "It's beautiful."

He tilted his head and gave a frustrated purse of his lips. "I thought it would bring out the green of your eyes, but these street lights aren't helping."

Oh, my.

"I suppose we'll have to go out tomorrow so I can see." He gestured to a police car when it pulled up.

"What's going on?" she asked, the intriguing promise of going out with him again being quickly replaced by a building panic.

"He's giving us a ride to my car."

Isabelle let out the breath she was holding and climbed in the back seat. She was further relieved when Matteo got in next to her; it eased the worry that something nefarious was happening.

A glance at the dashboard clock revealed it was twelve thirty.

"Thank you for coming to get me." Now she felt she could truly apologize.

"Do you think I'm the kind of man who would allow the reason for the best evening I've had in a very long time to be taken to jail without a goodnight kiss?"

She snorted, shaking her head. "Do you know, when I saw you as I was being driven away, I knew you'd help me."

"Did you?"

"Well, I couldn't be sure, but I had a feeling that whatever your job with the intelligence agency, you're one of the good guys."

"I am." He winked.

"Okay." She took a deep inhale and let it out slowly before holding out her hand. "Hi, I'm Isabelle Miller from Chicago. I'm a forensic anthropologist and I've been hired for the year to help with a dig in Rome through the American Academy."

"So we will be in the same city for a year?"

She shrugged.

He took her hand. "Matteo Arcuri." He said his name smoothly, probably the way he'd said it most of his life, only in Isabelle's head she swooned and slowly drawled, *'Oh, yes you are.'* "I work for the

Department of Information Security."

"Sounds ominous."

He smiled. "It would be a similar department as your CIA. I work to orchestrate operations between many of Italy's intelligence agencies."

"You said you were here working and for Christmas?" Isabelle asked.

"It's a small case, and since I was in the area ..." He reached out and touched the side of her face. "I had not planned to meet someone."

Isabelle's breath caught, and she thought, who cared if her second kiss was in the back of a police car. It seemed like just the perfect ending to such an unexpected turn of events this evening. But a thread of embarrassment was riding higher than the sexual tension so she forewent leaning into Matteo and instead asked, "What do I have to do for community service? And who assigned that? I thought only a judge could assign something like that."

"Well, when you know the right people, there is a way to hurry innocent situations along. Tomorrow you will have to go to the small town of Fiesole and help clean the trash that has gathered around the outdoor areas of the Museo Civico Archeologico."

"Museo?" she repeated.

"Yes," he tried to look contrite, "it's an archeological site with a Roman theater and Etruscan ruins ..." he trailed off, a sly grin in place.

"So for two hours I *have* to go see ruins?"

"And pick up trash."

"I see."

"And I have to go with you to make sure you abide by the agreement you entered into with the city of Florence."

She shook her head. "Smooth."

"I thought so."

The car pulled to a stop by the apartment building and Matteo thanked the officer, then saw Isabelle into his car. They didn't speak much as the car warmed up and Matteo maneuvered through the now empty streets.

"Are you okay? I can't imagine how uncomfortable you must be."

"Well, actually, I'm almost dry, but I don't think I smell very good."

"I'll get you back to the villa and help heat everything up."

Isabelle laughed and waved a hand at Matteo's questioning look; she wasn't going to tell him what thought ran through her mind. But, it was almost one in the morning, she was with a veritable stranger who just saved her from being kicked out of Florence because she fell into an iconic fountain (that none of the locals ever really liked, she reminded an invisible jury). Also, he'd kissed her, setting up a longing for him in her chest, and since he definitely had an easygoing sense of humor, she figured ...

"I was thinking of all the things you seem to have been very good at tonight; heating things up seems to be your specialty."

Chapter 8

The villa might have been colder inside than it was outside.

Isabelle handed Matteo the two laminated pages that explained how to use certain features of the villa.

He tapped them against his leg and gave her an apologetic look. "Unfortunately, we cannot turn the heater on right now."

"We can't turn it on right now," she repeated with a frown.

"Italy has heating laws from November to April. These heaters can only be turned on from five in the morning until eleven at night."

"And now that it's way past eleven …" she filled in. "Does the water heater work that way?"

"No, it shouldn't." He read through the pages and asked, "Do you know where the water heater is?"

"I don't. I'm not even sure where to begin to look, but if you need someone to have extensive knowledge about the structure, variations, and characteristics of human bones, give me a call." She chuckled but when Matteo angled his head and narrowed his gaze, she mirrored his study and asked, "Yes?"

"Nothing." His intensity was replaced with a grin as he said, "You are fascinating." He dropped the pages on the table and nodded. "Let's find the water heater."

They looked in every closet and when they didn't find it, began to open every door, cupboard and drawer in the place. When they still couldn't find it, Matteo said, "Now we look outside."

Led by the flashlight from his cell phone, they finally found a small dilapidated external closet. When the door gave an eerie creak as it was opened, Isabelle laughed and stood closer to Matteo's back, explaining,

"Just make sure the Italian Christmas ghosts get you first."

"They don't show up until the twenty-third."

"Really?"

There was a smile in his voice when he answered, "No."

His flashlight illuminated the blessed water heater and after he opened the panel he nodded. "The light is out. Do you have any matches or a lighter?"

"There are matches by the fireplace," she said, but didn't move. When he turned to look at her, she said, "It's kinda dark."

"Do you have your phone?"

"It's dead."

He handed his over. "I'll stay out here with the ghosts, you get the matches in the house, but don't let the Christmas goblins get you."

She clicked her tongue and muttered as she left him.

When she returned with matches, it took several tries before the pilot light whooshed into action.

"Good, that should fix the hot water problem. But first, we need to turn on a faucet to test it."

Back inside, Isabelle turned on the kitchen faucet as Matteo explained, "It usually only takes two or three minutes."

It took five.

But when the water began to run hot Isabelle excitedly asked, "Will I be able to take a hot shower? Right now?"

He nodded and she sighed, happy to finally find some warmth somewhere and get rid of what she could only refer to as the 'wet dog' smell.

"I'm going to go ..." She licked her lips and crossed the space that separated them; patting his chest she softly said, "Don't ... go anywhere."

"I had not planned on it." His lowered voice helped warm the room.

Showered and clean, but most importantly *warm*; Isabelle brushed her hair, pinched her cheeks, decided to forego formality and paired long yoga pants with a soft pink sweater, then grabbed the comforter off her bed.

When she entered the living room, the lights had been turned off and Matteo was sitting on the sofa. The fire he'd built was roaring with life and had pushed some of the cold air away, its emanating golden light causing the two glasses of wine he'd poured and set on the coffee table to glow.

Soft jazzy music from the stereo in the kitchen drifted around to bring the decadent scene to its pinnacle.

When he saw her, he sat forward and picked up a glass to hand her. She put the comforter on the back of the sofa, accepted the glass and didn't give her urge to cuddle up next to him another thought. When he draped his arm around her shoulders, the move felt so familiar and so very inviting.

"Do you feel better?"

"So much better." She took a sip and sighed, letting her bones melt into the sofa and Matteo's warmth. "Though, I think I need to get your coat dry cleaned for you. It smells like ... wet tourist."

His whole body shook as he laughed, and he squeezed her shoulders. "We'll just let it air out. I'm sure it will be fine.

Do they have Febreze in Italy? she wondered.

"I have to thank you," Matteo said softly.

"For what?"

"The most entertaining night I've had in a long time."

"As you said earlier, I'm happy to help." And then because she just needed to hear herself say it, added, "Though I am sorry."

"I am too."

"What are you sorry for?"

"I have not yet told you, there were several people who saw the entire event. They knew you were just trying to help and told the Carabinieri."

"But that's a good thing, isn't it? I was worried that everyone thought I was just some ugly American tourist disgracing Italy's art."

"There were those who did not see the whole event, and probably wondered why you chose such a cold night to jump in—"

"Is that what you thought?" She leaned back so she could look into his eyes.

"I didn't know what to think. But I gave you the benefit of the doubt." She grunted and he pulled her back against him. "I'm trying to apologize, because I could have gotten you out of the station earlier."

"Okay ..."

He quickly explained, "The Carabinieri suggested that making you wait, might help to make sure you would never do such a thing ever again."

Isabelle's eyes widened and she sat up once more to glare at him. "I'm not planning on jumping in any more fountains or ever again helping any more children who throw things into them," she insisted.

Of course, several of her nephews and nieces' faces floated past her and she thought, *except them, I'd probably jump into a fountain for them.*

"A forensic anthropologist. That sounds fascinating," Matteo said.

In an attempt to sound contrite, she responded, "Nice change of subject ..." But quickly gave up as she settled into his warmth and he began to knead the back of her neck.

"It's a fascinating job."

"Well," she put her feet on the coffee table, "*I* think so, but it's not as interesting as people think. I *have* worked with the police on a handful of cold cases over the years, but for the most part, I work in correlation with museums and university funded labs."

"How did you decide on that career path?"

"Actually, it's my mom's fault. She's a dental hygienist and when I was about eleven, she came home from work and told us about how she helped the police in an investigation. That was the first time I found out how dental records were used to identify someone and what forensic sciences were all about. I was hooked."

They fell silent while the wine and music eased away the rough edges of the evening. Finally warm all over, Isabelle gave into the yawn that she'd been trying to hold back.

"I'm very tired," she admitted to Matteo, "and I don't want to keep you but ..."

She could feel his breath against her ear. "You're keeping me exactly where I want to be." That deep accent enticed an eruption in her chest.

When his lips brushed a kiss just below her ear, she naturally bent her head to the side; just in case he needed to continue his assault on her neck. And as he did, she sighed and yawned again. "I'm sorry, it's not you. I'm just so comfortable and warm and ..." She didn't continue her explanation, but instead put her empty glass on the table and stood.

Matteo was about to object until she turned and boldly placed a knee on either side of his hips then sat on his lap, facing him.

His hands greedily reached for her hips and pulled her as close as he could before she lowered her lips against his and the kiss that began in the piazza was reignited.

Isabelle had a faint thought that while first kisses were delightful – that first brush of lips together, the first taste, the initial excitement; second kisses, the real kisses, when hands roam freely and breathing turns shallow, were downright magical.

The rhythm between them was tingling as dizziness bounced and twirled inside and out; and shivers and trembling were no longer from the cold in the air, but the heat building between them and their desires were constructed through need, because just pressing bodies together wasn't enough.

The kissing had become otherworldly and still she wanted more; they both did. Which was evident when Matteo's full strength was realized as he lifted Isabelle up and laid her back on the sofa, covering her with his body in a split second. And still clad in all their clothes, they reconnected in the most natural tangle of tongues and fingers and exploration.

Matteo was a gentle force while Isabelle was demanding. She wrapped herself up in his kisses, opening her mouth to him; and as she met another sweep of his tongue, she drowned in the taste of late night wine and espresso.

They moaned and moved against each other until their lips fell away because they'd gone so long without breathing. And that's when exhaustion and jet lag were expressed through shared yawns; causing them both to laugh softly.

Matteo shifted her once again, positioning her in front of him as they lay on their sides so they could both fit on the sofa. Holding her against his chest, he reached up and pulled the comforter over them.

And in the dying light of the fire, Isabelle's eyes fluttered closed to the deep whisper of "Buonanotte, bella."

Chapter 9

The screaming of a phone woke Isabelle; that, and Matteo launching himself into an upright position, caused her to roll off the limited space the sofa offered onto the floor.

They both cursed, and as Isabelle tried to catch herself, Matteo also lunged for her, causing them both to end up on the floor, Matteo on top. But it was far from some romantic morning playfulness as Isabelle was face down and Matteo, trying to catch her and not squish her, slammed his side against the hard floor beneath the rug and the rest of him into the coffee table. The table took offense and tried to move out of the way, knocking over a wine glass that had a sip of wine left and, missing Matteo, spilled onto Isabelle's backside.

"No," she moaned into the rug as Matteo finished calling her name in an attempt to stop the entire string of events that had just occurred. And the phone gave up attempting to get his attention.

"Isabella?" he said concerned, as he pushed the table out of the way to free himself from his position and help her up. "Are you okay?"

She held Matteo's hand while she craned her neck to see how bad the stain on her backside was, because it felt substantial.

The phone began screaming again and Isabelle shook her head as a laugh bubbled up, then she patted his cheek. "Answer your phone. I need to go put a different pair of pants on."

As she headed to her room, she heard him answer, "Pronto?"

She shivered as she shuffled into the room, it was cold again. After opting for jeans, taking time to brush her teeth and hair, she made the mistake of splashing her face with ice cold water; but at least it gave her some lovely color.

On her return, she picked up the scarf Matteo had bought her from the edge of one of the overstuffed chairs in the living room, shook it out to its full length and used it as a shawl. The next order of business, she figured, was coffee.

She pulled out the espresso she'd bought along with the supplied espresso maker (that Angela had thankfully explained when she was first showing Isabelle around) just as Matteo ended his conversation with "sì, sì, sì, ciao ciao, ciao."

He crossed the room and leaned his hip against the counter as she turned on the burner. "Isabella, how do you feel about children's dance recitals?"

"I have four nieces, three in dance. So I suppose the quick answer is that I am the world's best aunt because I tolerate them perfectly."

"And how would you feel about joining me to see the dance recital for two of my nipoti today?"

"Sure." She tried to ignore the way her mouth dried at the implication of the invitation. "When is it?"

He glanced at the phone, giving a lopsided grin. "In forty-five minutes."

"What? What time is it now?"

"It's ten fifteen."

She shook her head. "I haven't slept that long in a while."

"Being arrested is exhausting," he teased.

She pointed a warning finger at him. "Too soon." She winked, then suggested, "It's the jet lag. And I was finally warm."

"Ah, yet again, Matteo comes to the rescue to heat you up."

She cleared her throat on the many, *many* responses that came to mind but just grinned at him. He mirrored her reaction, causing the first glimmer of a game of 'Chicken' to have been established, but the gurgle of the espresso maker announcing it was almost done waylaid any advances.

Isabelle gingerly opened the lid, found it full of liquid, and turned off the burner. "So we need to hurry?" she asked as she began making a mental list of what she'd need to do to get ready, and what she'd need to pack if she was going to do her 'community service' later in the day. It probably didn't make sense to come all the way back here.

Matteo made a sound as he shrugged and opened a cupboard to liberate two espresso cups. "Sit down, we'll have a coffee first," he said as he divided the heavenly liquid.

"Won't we be late?" she asked as she sat at the head of the table. "And just to check, you know we just met and you're inviting me to a family event."

"I realize this."

"And you're still sure you want me to go?"

"I worry that if you don't come with me, you'll end up in trouble again."

A grunt was her reply.

"It's just a dance recital. We can watch and then leave. Then I can tell my family I was there and I won't get in trouble."

He brushed a kiss on her cheek then sat down next to her.

"Maybe I should meet you at the museum after instead ..." The idea had merit, even more so after she voiced it. That's what she'd do. She was getting ready to explain her plan but he picked up his phone and made a call.

After a laughing conversation and departing "ciao," he explained, "My nieces are the tenth and fifteenth to perform. We have plenty of time."

"You don't want to be there for the whole show?"

"There has been a summer and winter dance recital for the past eight years," he gave a sighing shrug, "there will be more." He picked up his cup and continued, "We have time and will still arrive in time to see them dance."

She still wasn't so sure she'd be going with him. "Do you want something to eat then?"

"We'll stop on the way and grab a pastry."

"We will?"

"Certo." He leaned across the distance that separated them, gently caressed her cheek and offered a deep, temptation-building whisper, "Good morning, bella."

She let herself drown in the moment as she breathed, "Buongiorno."

So ... it looked like she was going to see his nieces and possibly meet a stray family member or two.

That was fine.

Right?

She was a new friend who was alone on Christmas. And this was the kind of thing new friends did.

Right?

Back in the car and headed back to Florence through the winding roads of the Tuscan countryside, Isabelle watched the magical scenery as it passed. There were dark shadows of trees that had lost their leaves; slight hills where farmland, resting for the winter, had become rolling carpets of velvety wheat color; rows of sleeping grapevines adding dark maroon colors; and olive trees that winked a silver hue. And finally, large cypress and Italian pine trees rounded out the pallet with their dark greens.

The car was warm, but the morning cold and humid air fogged up the windows.

Isabelle had quickly dumped out everything from her overnight bag she'd used on the plane and repacked it with a shirt she could collect trash in, some makeup, and another outfit – just in case her good Samaritan nature took hold and she ended up jump-falling into another body of water.

Her phone beeped and she read the update from her brother. It was still snowing, but the storm was supposed to break tomorrow. The airline had not changed their original updates, so the family should be able to make it out on Monday.

Two more days.

But that wasn't as depressing as it had been when she first arrived. After all, she'd found a handsome way to bide her time. And he spoke the language and knew the area, so it was a win-win.

Of course, the fact that he was handy in tricky situations didn't hurt; nor did the fact that she really enjoyed his company. *And be honest,* she chided herself; she wanted to make out with this man a lot more and find out what other 'handy tricks' he had at his disposal.

A bundle of emotions thrilled through her bloodstream at the very thought.

She shifted in her seat as they stopped at the first light on the 'outskirts' of the city.

Soon traffic would compound itself. Isabelle studied the shops and apartments as they blinked by and craned her neck to take in the river while they crossed a bridge. After a few more confusing turns, Matteo pulled down an apartment lined street and parked awkwardly on a corner. He turned on his hazard lights before turning off the car, then rounded to Isabelle's door.

"What's going on?" she asked, accepting his hand.

"We need a little something to eat." He gestured to the café he'd pulled up next to.

She glanced at the car, then around at the street with vehicles overstuffed in every spot available for parking. "You can park here?"

"Ah, we won't be that long," he urged.

She thanked him when he held the door open and checked her watch. It was five minutes until the start of the recital. "Your family won't be mad that you're late?" she asked once more.

"No," he waved the idea away, "as long as I see my nieces dance." He nodded to the case of glistening pastries. "What looks good?"

"All of them," she sighed. And if he meant for the warmth of the café and the aromatic smells to douse any further talk about propriety of time … well, it worked.

A symphony of clinking cups and spoons being set upon saucers accompanied the steaming of milk and smells of sweet pastry and coffee.

She pointed to a sticky roll with a sign in Italian, but it wasn't too far of a leap to understand it contained 'pistacchio.'

"Cappuccino or espresso?" he asked.

"Cappuccino."

Orders taken, Isabelle followed him to the end of the bar where the barista was working. He nodded at them, set two saucers on the counter, magically produced two cappuccinos, added spoons, then slid the gloriousness across to them with little ceremony before starting on the next order.

She leaned her hip against the bar, mirroring Matteo and the other customers who were taking sips and bites; not rushing, but not lingering.

She sighed. "I think I love this most of all."

"After a year in Roma, you will be an expert," he supplied matter-of-factly.

She stilled her cup and stared off into the distance at his comment. It wasn't real yet, that she wasn't going home after this. That a furnished apartment and a new adventure awaited her.

"A year in Rome," she muttered.

The decision had been an academic one. There was experience to be gained and it was an amazing offer.

But now, sipping a cappuccino with locals, it was a different excitement that unexpectedly took hold.

"I need to learn the language," she stated.

"Were you not planning on learning it?" Matteo teased.

"I was, they said there was a program I would attend ... but now ..." she glanced around her and then up at Matteo, "I think I want to learn it faster."

"Okay," he rubbed his hands free of crumbs, "sei affascinante." He said the phrase slowly.

"Say," she tried and he nodded for her to continue, "a fashee non tay?"

He winked and gave a cocky, "I know."

"What?" She shook her head in confusion.

"You said I was fascinating."

She rolled her eyes and he stepped toward her, slipped his arm around her waist and as his mouth slowly inched its way to hers, whispered, "Sei molto affascinante."

She smiled just before she melted against him and offered her own whisper of "Smooth."

Chapter 10

B eing raised so close to Chicago, with parents who were insistent
that their children have an appreciation of the arts, Isabelle had
been to her fair share of theater. And even though this was a children's
dance recital, it was quite reminiscent of intermissions at most theater
shows, when the smokers, and a few others, gathered outside for the
break. And while there were a few people smoking nearby, she was
shocked at the number of people visiting, pacing or talking on phones
outside the venue of the recital.

She followed Matteo into the auditorium where a loud blast of music
greeted them and after a quick visit with a couple leaving, he turned to
explain, "Perfect, this is number eight."

He took the first seats he found and Isabelle was charmed at how
halfway around the world, some things weren't that different. Proud
parents waved in the darkness as preschool-aged kids, dressed as fairies,
awkwardly tried to float across the stage in unison.

The backdrop was a bright, squat, cartoon forest, and Isabelle
assumed it was the theme that would tie the whole performance together.
But as one number moved into the next, the theme lost any cohesion.

A group of tap dancing Santas shuffled off only to be replaced by
blooming dandelions (one of which was Matteo's niece). But then
pandas came into play followed by a hip-hop group of sailors.

"Matteo," she whispered to get his attention, "is there some Italian
Christmas fairy tale with sailors, fairies, Santa and pandas?"

He shook his head. "I don't remember any."

His other niece was in the next group (maybe third grade, all dressed
as different fruits. Isabelle smiled and wondered when the last time was

that anyone had seen a pineapple in the forest).

When the number was over, Matteo gave a loud whistle of appreciation as they joined their clapping with the rest of the audience. When the dancers exited, he leaned over and whispered, "Want to leave?"

"Are we allowed to?" It was a ridiculous question, but seriously, were they allowed to? Because her older brother would have given her such crap if she'd come late and only stayed for her nieces' numbers then left early.

Even as she asked the question, she rolled her eyes at herself and knew the reaction was a throwback to her Catholic upbringing. Going late to Mass and leaving early was a dire no-no. (Of course, those rules loosened up a bit as everyone got older. And as far as she knew, if any of her siblings were still going to church, it was only on the high holy days. Easter and Christmas. Arriving late and leaving early. So why were the recitals different?)

Matteo took her hand in answer to her question and as he walked nonchalantly, Isabelle ducked slightly as they walked up the aisle, a combination of guilt and trying to make sure she wasn't in anyone's eyeline.

"I'm going to immediately start implementing an 'only watching my nieces' numbers' policy," she said under her breath as they followed another wave of family leaving through the main doors.

"They were darling," Isabelle commented when they were outside, but Matteo wasn't listening. He stopped their progress and when glancing up at him, she found his jaw clenching, his attention on something ahead of them.

She followed his line of sight and was surprised to find that his reaction might be due to a grinning group of spectators, six in all, who were vying for his attention.

When one of them waved, "O, Matteo!" there was no question about it.

"Perhaps we should have stayed inside," he muttered.

"Oh, no." She shook her head, enjoying his discomfort; probably because so far, he had a certainty and ease about him, so this sudden *unease* was interesting. "I think this is *exactly* where we should be." She took a step, and because he didn't move and they were still holding hands, had to tug him into action.

Matteo grunted and may have slouched his shoulders slightly, but grudgingly followed.

The group met them halfway, and the attention their clasped hands was receiving wasn't lost on Isabelle. But once they were within range, everyone spoke at once and as questions were volleyed, Matteo said one phrase above the din, "Questa è Isabella." Then she was passed from person to person with a hearty squeeze of the shoulders and kisses planted on her cheeks.

When the whirlwind was over, he worked his way right to left and introduced his various family members: a brother and his wife, his sister and her husband, another sister-in-law, and his father.

"We apologize," the spokesperson, Matteo's sister Sara, finally raised her voice above the group, "Babbeo has never brought a woman home for Christmas."

"She is not *brought home* for Christmas," he mumbled, causing his sister to face him and reach up to pinch both of his cheeks as she cooed, "Ovviamente no. Of course not, Matteo Babbeo."

He slapped at his sister's hands and was promptly placed in a headlock by one of the men who reiterated a cooing, "O, Babbeo."

"What does that mean?" Isabelle asked Sara, her grin widening from this entertaining glimpse into Matteo's family life.

Sara explained, "It's a term of endearment, but you do not want to call anyone you just met this word. It means stupid."

Isabelle scrunched her face. "Stupid?"

Sara wiggled her head and tented her fingers together. "Yes, but in a tender way. Because the word has a rhyme and for a time, Matteino was the baby of the family."

"I'm not ..." Matteo twisted, turning the headlock around so his brother was under his elbow; then before letting him go, he kissed his brother's head and backed up, brushing his hand over his coat. "I'm actually the second born."

Sara continued her sisterly humiliation, "But he was *so* small for *so* long. We worried he would never grow into a man. And now that he has, we have been worried he would *never* find a woman. But I think that is about to change too?"

Matteo sighed. "Isabella is a friend visiting Firenze, and her family has not arrived yet because they are stuck in a snowstorm," he said then repeated the excuse in Italian.

It was received with tisks of reproach.

The brother drew out her name, "Isabella" and then continued in Italian as he gestured between the two.

Isabelle glanced at Sara for a translation.

"The way Babbeo says your name, it is not the way a man would say your name if he was *just* a friend. And you were holding hands—"

"We have to go," Matteo interrupted.

"We do?" Isabelle asked.

"Isabella has community service she must do."

She tilted her head, eyes wide; stupid indeed. She smiled as she whispered, "You invited *me* to this lovely recital with your family and now you're gonna throw me under the bus?"

"What bus?" he asked.

"I haven't met the whole family yet, have I?" She didn't wait for him to answer and repeated the question, louder, to Sara, "I haven't met the whole family yet, have I?"

Sara beamed. "No, you have not."

All the while Isabelle was involved in the English part of the conversation, an animated Italian version was happening with Matteo and the rest of his family.

"Will you come for lunch?" Sara asked. "You can meet everyone." But before Isabelle could answer Matteo said, "O, Sara, domani or dopo domani, okay?"

"Perché?"

"What?" Isabelle asked.

Matteo sighed as he admitted in a soft tone, "I want to spend the day with *you*, not with you and my family."

She grinned. "But if *I* want to have lunch with your family ...?"

Sara laughed, translating, and Isabelle was enjoying the appreciative nods she received.

Matteo snarled at the happy group. "Tomorrow. We'll come to lunch tomorrow."

Isabelle leaned into his side and asked, "So you want to see me tomorrow too?" She was pretty sure her words were translated and that was why a hush fell over his family.

He squared himself to her, glanced once over his shoulder at his family, then let a smile replace his frustration. "I really do."

"Good." She aimed a smile at Sara. "Unfortunately, we won't be able to make it for lunch today, but if it isn't too much of an inconvenience, I'd love to visit with everyone tomorrow."

His brother pulled Matteo into his side, slapping his chest a few times as he inserted another round of ribbing.

Sara reiterated, "He's never brought a woman home before."

Isabelle had a passing thought about the possibility of introducing Matteo to her family; it wouldn't be much different than this. She felt at home in this moment and thought, without a doubt, he'd be right at home among her familial mayhem.

Sara reached out and gently squeezed Isabelle's forearm. "So maybe he's not so stupid after all."

Chapter 11

After more confusing twists and turns – that made it feel like they were somehow doubling back to their original starting point at the villa – they were once again, creeping out of the confines of the city, up into the hills surrounding Florence.

Matteo pulled off the main road, onto a long, packed dirt driveway, past hibernating trees and bushes before finally parking next to a stone wall covered in twisted ivy overgrowth.

When he didn't turn the car off but instead, stared out the window with a frown, she raised an eyebrow. "Matteo?"

"I need to change my clothes," he said.

She nodded and waited. He turned the car off and checked his phone. "We probably have thirty minutes, but I only need fifteen."

"Why do you only have thirty minutes to change your clothes?" She followed him out of the car. He gestured to a break in the wall where she could see long, gradually declining stairsteps that formed more of a ramp; which led to a yard next to a three-story, stone house.

"Are we breaking in?" she tried to joke.

"Kind of …" Matteo waited a few beats and then sighed. "This is my parents' house. Where I'm staying while I'm in town."

"Is this where you grew up?" she asked delightedly.

He frowned but gave a nod.

"The ancestral home." Isabelle skipped the rest of the way to the bottom of the stairs to the red, bricked driveway that surrounded the house. "Why didn't you park here?"

"Easy escape up there." He jerked his head upward.

"Your family seems very nice," Isabelle said.

Matteo barked out a laugh. "That is true. They do *seem* nice." He unlocked the door and stood aside, allowing Isabelle in first. It wasn't the front door he'd opened, but the door to the kitchen.

"Make yourself at home." He took off his camel coat and hung it on the back of one of the chairs slid against the long lace covered table in the dining area, where he then tossed his wallet, phone and keys. "I'll be quick," he added; only he was facing away from her and already pulling his sweater over his head to reveal a very attractive group of muscles flexing as he walked away.

"Oh ... my," she whispered to herself and then rolled her eyes and chided, "Izzy, that is *exactly* what got us in this situation to begin with."

Of course, her *self* grinned; *it isn't that bad a situation though, is it?*

She turned a circle and surveyed the stone walls, terracotta floors and dark wood beams on the ceiling. The large open space encompassed the living room, dining room and kitchen.

She crossed to the living room, reaching out to touch the branches of a small Christmas tree that stood in front of the television. Parallel sofas, with a coffee table between them, offered everyone the heat from the fireplace. The entire home was brimming with generations of family, their history steeped into the very walls.

But it was the three arched windows, shutters open, allowing the daylight in, that Isabelle thought were the most important element of this house. Because they offered a gorgeous, spectacular, panoramic view of Florence.

Green cypress and fir trees edged the city, and then, reaching into the sky were white and beige toned buildings topped with terracotta rooftops. The Duomo winked at her from where she preened in all her vast glory. It was an immense structure when standing up close, but from here, her intimidating frame was enhanced. Winter clouds rolled across the sky, creating a perfect backdrop for this city that had been on display for generations.

She sighed and began to hunt the walls hung with family photos and was delighted by awkward teenage Matteo, his lips pulled in a frustrated line. Then Matteo as a young man, all smiles this time. And a possible baby picture, but the four children looked so similar.

The shelving appeared to hold precious memories; vases and a gold framed photo of Mary alongside black and white photos of stoic looking men and women with this house in the background.

There were two dark wood hutches that housed various dishes, platters, glassware, and ceramic pitchers. Each one had a laminated card tucked into the edge where glass met wood, one of Jesus and another of a saint she didn't recognize.

Isabelle touched the lace on the back of the sofa as she crossed back to the windows; the view calling to her. She wasn't sure how long she stood there, but knew it wasn't more than fifteen minutes.

"Are you ready?" Matteo called from the hallway where he'd originally disappeared.

He wore a gray sweater and dark pants now. His hair was still wet, though given its mussy look, he'd obviously scrubbed it with a towel and then dressed. And somehow that made him look more delectable than when he brushed his hair into place. He had a scarf and another jacket draped over his arm.

"You weren't kidding about hurrying."

He sighed and put everything he carried on the edge of the sofa, then didn't stop until he'd wrapped a hand around Isbelle's waist and pulled her against him. "There are going to be so many questions, and if we get caught here, we won't leave for two days. Everyone will show up, neighbors and a few more aunts and uncles who live nearby and my mom won't stop cooking."

"That's a bad thing?" She breathed out the question because being pulled into his warm body, and the smell that wafted off of him, was intoxicating.

He dipped his head and brushed a gentle kiss on her lips, then pulled away and said, "I want you to myself for just a little more time."

"I mean, when you put it that way ..." She returned a quick kiss, pressed her hands against his chest and pushed him away, reasoning, "If you keep kissing me, we're never going to leave and then we'll get caught by your big bad family."

He gave her hands a squeeze in agreement then shuffled his phone, wallet and keys back in his pockets before pulling on his jacket and scarf.

"This is a lovely place to grow up," Isabelle declared as they started to leave.

"It was my great-great-grandfather's house on my father's side."

"So it really is the ancestral home."

He nodded. "Do your parents still live in the same house you grew up in?"

She shook her head. "No. They wanted something smaller."

When they arrived at the car Matteo looked relieved.

"The view from the living room is amazing," she offered.

"I'm sorry you weren't able to explore more. Maybe later."

He started the car and once more, they were off.

"Are you expecting me to introduce you to my family?" she asked.

"I think that would be nice."

"We'll see."

He pulled onto the main road, still heading up into the hills.

"It's kinda fun feeling like the girl who you're sneaking around with."

"You *are* the girl I'm sneaking around with."

"But I'm not bad for you," she reasoned. "I don't think…" And before he could reply she eyed him adding, "Whether you're good or bad for me remains to be seen."

Chapter 12

"That's it?" Isabelle asked, as she stood in the police station once more, signing her name to a document.

"That's it." Matteo read over the paper, gave a satisfied nod and slid it across the desk to the clerk whose frown increased. After a quick exchange and a stamp on the paper, the clerk growled at them both. Isabelle didn't even need to speak the language to know that meant 'go away and leave me alone.'

Outside, as they buttoned up jackets and adjusted scarves, Matteo elbowed Isabelle. "Now your debt has been paid."

"Some debt," she scoffed, "I picked up five wrappers in return for free entrance to the ruins and museum."

"Esattamente, no one else was going to pick up those five pieces of trash."

She shook her head. "You know, part of me wonders if you planted them."

"How? I was with you the whole time," he defended.

"Ah, but I'm not fluent in Italian, maybe you told the waiter at lunch to go toss a few wrappers around."

He chuckled, and Isabelle bumped him with her hip in reply. Because what she really wanted to do was wrap her arms around his neck, take those strong hands and place them around her waist and drown in him.

Her steady breathing hitched from the image and she took a shaky inhale; luckily, Matteo had been tucking his scarf into the top of his jacket and didn't notice.

"What will you do now that you are a free woman?" he asked, finally glancing at her.

She wiggled her eyebrows. "I'd like to go check out some more fountains."

"I have a better idea." He nodded down the street and Isabelle followed his direction.

Of course she would; at this point, following Matteo had led to some rather impressive sights and spectacular food. She never thought she was the kind of person who could be bribed with food, but if the meals continued to exceed expectation, well, bring on the bribery.

Beyond the food, there was a slow immersion into the culture she hadn't anticipated. And beyond *that*, was the pure pleasure of meeting someone who seemed to like her enough to want to get to know her, and who she liked enough to want to get to know better (of course the flirting, hand holding, intentional brush of hands against each other, and the building need to kiss him again and feel his hands on her body wasn't hurting anything either).

The sun had set, and gray clouds transformed into brushes of white against the twilight blue sky. The temperature dropped enough that she used it as an excuse to slip her arm through Matteo's, even though she didn't need an excuse. As he hugged her arm to his side, she felt this simple action, innocent really, had been something they'd done their whole lives.

When they turned a corner at the end of the street, she sighed; this wasn't bad either. In the city center, in the apex of it all, around each corner seemed to be a new wonder and she'd barely scratched the surface of exploration.

Matteo bent his head toward her. "I like when you sigh like that."

"I sighed?"

"In a way that tempts me."

Oh ...

She wasn't sure how to reply, which was fine because she was having a slight problem finding her voice.

He stopped their progress and bent his head toward her ear. "I would love nothing more than to make you sigh again and again and again."

... my.

He brushed a kiss on her temple before prodding them back into action. He'd fogged up her vision and made her dizzy, like she'd just gotten off the teacup ride at Disneyland; she was glad she could hold onto him.

Following the gleaming path painted before them, the soft conversation of pedestrians and their footsteps echoed off the close knit buildings.

Restaurants they passed were yawning awake, readying themselves for the coming diners.

Other stores had been closed for the evening, the gray guard gates shut and locked, leaving the quick bouts of bubbled and angled graffiti that began on the stucco walls to complete nonsensical sentences.

"I'm glad you feel that way," it was her turn to lean into him, "because since you took your sweater off and I saw the torso we're working with, I find I am *very* interested in running my hands ... " He slipped his hand around her waist and was facing her now, a widening grin, his eyebrows raised with interested expectation. She swallowed. "Well ..."

"Well?" he whispered, leaning down, his eyes searching hers, his lips close but waiting for her to finish her thought.

"Well ..." She grinned.

"Isabella?"

"Yeah?"

"What do you want to do with your hands and my body?"

She glanced at Matteo, everything about him was so inviting: olive skin, dark hair, carefully trimmed beard defining a strong jaw, full lips meant to be kissed and shoulders that held up quite a tempting frame.

Good lord.

She sighed and it was barely a whisper when she finished, "Explore every inch of you?"

He claimed her mouth in a kiss and using her hips as leverage, pulled her against him. Isabelle wrapped her arms around his neck and held on as the cold was deflected, the heat between them building fires of yearning and need.

The mad beep of a car forced them apart. Matteo shook his head as he still held her, but when another beep came, he turned to the vehicle – a taxi trying to get through – and with one hand on Isabelle's waist, the other tented backwards, he laughingly shook it at the offending vehicle. "Oh! You can not give me one moment for passion?!"

A matching hand flicked out the driver side window with garbled sentiment, but they moved out of the way and the taxi gave another beep as he passed them.

Matteo slipped her arm once more into the crook of his and they continued their meander over ancient bricks, led by the glow of strung twinkle lights above.

As they turned a corner, Isabelle wasn't disappointed that it gave way to a piazza that contained a sea of covered stalls lit with strands of lightbulbs, against the backdrop of another intimidating historic cathedral.

"Wow."

"The Christmas Market," Matteo introduced.

Now *this* was the Christmas she expected from Europe. The kind shown in movies and travel documentaries. The closest stall had a fan propelling the heat from an outdoor oven in their direction, and the smell of cinnamon and sugar and pastry was captivating.

The buildings that surrounded the piazza were covered with similar color light projections they'd seen the previous evening.

Had that been just yesterday?

She slipped her arm down to find his hand, then with a jerk of her head in the direction of the stalls, did a slight skip and pulled him to follow her.

Florence already had her senses on overload, and Matteo pushed everything into overdrive; so this cheerfully crowded, dazzling, sensory filled market was the cherry to top it all.

Rows were set up neatly with enough room to create an aisle for all the bundled shoppers. Live music was floating from places unseen. The air was filled with spices and warmth.

Stalls were impressively stacked with goods. After glancing at the first few booths, she said, "It has a German feel."

Matteo nodded. "Yes, you will see a lot of Swiss, Dutch and German items."

It was a treasure trove of handmade crafts and artisan work. Dried flower arrangements, soaps, handblown glass, jewelry and a booth that glowed with strands of lighted paper stars and lanterns.

A Scotland booth was bedecked with plaid, and the British

representation had ceramic plates and platters on display next to pretty teapots and teacups with matching saucers stacked on top of each other.

There were dried fruits, spices and candy. Macaroons and chocolate. Dipped waffles and pastries; so many pastries it seemed irresponsible not to buy at least a dozen.

However, when it came to finally purchasing a souvenir, it was an Italian booth with hanging red baubles that beckoned her closer.

Various hand-painted ceramic ornaments sparkled. They showed Tuscan scenes, a lot of olive branches, and most bore the sentiment 'Buon Natale.' But it was one in particular that captured all her attention; a charming villa in the countryside, so reminiscent of her current address, painted butter yellow in the background, and on the opposite side, a branch of olives.

She picked up the box it was in and handed it over to the vendor. Matteo was pulling out his wallet, but Isabelle put her hand on his sleeve to stop him. He seemed to understand she wanted to buy *this* for herself.

Her treasure was added to the bag holding pastries and they continued.

Santa, a thinner version than that from America, in a floor-length, velvet maroon coat called out greetings as he walked through the crowd, followed by a barrage of children yelling their excitement.

A slight breeze pushed the smell of roasted chestnuts into their path just as the bells of the church began to ring.

Isabelle stopped, raising an eyebrow at Matteo. "Are you kidding me?" she asked excitedly.

"I'm glad this worked out. Tomorrow is the last day the Market is open," he replied.

"No. Really? My family would've loved this." She glanced around as the bells, ringing a deep tone, still continued to fill the air. She suddenly found that she was taking mental notes, so she could tell her family what it was like.

Matteo assured her, "There is still plenty your family will find to do in this city."

He gestured to a hexagon shaped booth standing apart from the others. "Do you want some wine? It is warm with spices."

"Mulled wine?" She nodded and as if in a trance, made her way to the edge and smiled in greeting. Even though the woman asked a question in Italian, Isabelle gave a quick nod, certain she was being offered a glass.

The warm cup was handed over and this time she let Matteo pay. She took a sip; a delicate, sweet, and slight tartness with warm spices made her close her eyes and sigh.

So she wasn't aware that Matteo had moved so close to her ear until he whispered, "You must stop doing that," then nipped playfully at her earlobe, sending a shiver down that side of her body.

She opened her eyes and turned so she could give an innocent bat of her eyelashes as she took a breath and exhaled a very deep sigh. Matteo growled under his breath and rolled his eyes.

Laughing, Isabelle elbowed him and prodded them back into motion. "C'mon, there's more to see."

It began to rain, bringing an end to the evening for many of the visitors. Matteo bought an umbrella and Isabelle wondered if he bought just the one so they could continue their intimate proximity.

"Are you hungry?" he asked. They'd had a few decadent snacks while they walked the Market, but it wasn't a full meal.

"Do you have a place in mind?"

"Certo," he said, "but it is a little walk. I can find a taxi if you would like."

"I don't mind walking."

And she didn't. It was almost seven, so streets were empty of pedestrians, many having gone to dinner or choosing to stay out of the cool, rainy evening. Other than the downtown spectacle of the Market and lights in the various piazzas they'd visited; there didn't seem to be a rush. There was no sense of hurrying to buy and wrap; even her visit to the large grocery store had more of a relaxed atmosphere.

Or maybe it was just her current situation and Matteo that made her feel that way. Because as it was, she felt like she was floating through a dream, her feet barely aware of all the walking they'd done in just two days.

The wash of rain painted a sheen of enchantment on the cobblestones and Isabelle had barely blinked her eyes when the 'bit of a walk' was almost over and they were crossing the Ponte Vecchio.

The slight rise of the bridge was made ethereal by the glow of lights from shops on either side spilling onto the worn stones. It was everything she imagined it would be, but she had anticipated a sea of tourists, and there were only a handful. She and Matteo were virtually alone.

The shops – an array of jewelry and leather – were small, sardined together. Most had space inside for three, maybe five people. Some had their doors open, inviting last minute shoppers. Others were already closed for the night.

When they arrived at the center of the bridge there was a statue to the right, and a covered portico on the left. The wind blew slightly through at this point without any resistance from buildings, but at least it was dry.

Isabelle stepped away from Matteo and shook a few droplets off her jacket, her eyes taking in the lights of the buildings reflecting on either side of the Arno River. She beamed her smile at Matteo; his response was a narrowed gaze and darkening of his eyes as he unceremoniously dropped the umbrella to the ground, crossed the distance she'd placed between them, pressed his hand gently on her stomach as he forced her back, one, two, three steps, until her back came in contact with a pillar. He moved both his hands to cup her face, shook his head once studying her, then dipped his lips to hers. Isabelle dropped her bag of treasures and grappled for Matteo, giving in to the moment with abandon.

He brushed a hot kiss against her jaw and whispered her name, "Isabella." Just that one word, elongated, in a deep tone, carried on the breeze around her body and somehow held a lifetime of need within it.

Then his phone rang.

But they ignored it and continued to allow the heated passion to build.

It rang again.

The third time, he grunted angrily and pressed his forehead against hers. "Mi dispiace." He fumbled for his phone, and when he saw who was calling said, "I'm sorry. Work."

He didn't let her go, but held her in place during a quick conversation. But whatever the inconvenience was, his demeanor changed quickly and he straightened, touching the back of his hand to her cheek but no longer seeing her.

She knew the call probably had something to do with the 'pickpocket case.' He verified it as he ended the call with a frustrated growl of, "That was the officer I've been working with."

"You need to go," she filled in.

"I don't want to." He was back, eyes focused on her.

"I don't want you to go either," she pulled him down and brushed a soft kiss on his lips, "but I have a feeling it's important."

He nodded, pulling away and retrieving the umbrella and her bag. "The man we've been looking for has been spotted."

He handed both things over to her. "I'll get you a taxi." He glanced in each direction of the bridge as if he didn't recall where they were or which direction they'd been heading. He looked back and once again reached out and touched the side of her face. "I am truly sorry."

If he continued to mindlessly touch her face and look at her as if she were precious, wearing his need so blatantly on his face, Isabelle wasn't sure she'd ever be able to complete a sensible sentence again. Still, as he apologized, she was pretty sure she could hold him to one truth. "I have a feeling you'll make it up to me."

He winked, made another call and after hanging up said, "There is a bar on the other side of the bridge. The taxi will pick us up there." They began to walk and he apologized again, "I am sorry."

"Matteo, you said you're here working. You didn't anticipate entertaining ... company ..." She wasn't necessarily company, but she didn't know how to define herself at the moment.

"I–"

"Get your phone back out."

He gave her a confused look but followed directions.

She explained, "I don't have your number. And you don't have mine."

After numbers were exchanged, the taxi arrived. They rode part way together, and when it stopped to let Matteo out, he kissed Isabelle; the kind of kiss that sealed the promise that he would indeed make up for this. And Isabelle wasn't sure she even blinked away the passion of that intention until the taxi pulled in front of the Casa Villa.

She floated inside and when the cold embraced her, began to laugh. She still hadn't figured out the heating and the one man who was doing a very good job of keeping her warm was otherwise engaged.

She opted for a hot shower, and her laughter grew as the hot water heater appeared to be out again.

So she was left with starting a fire, and *that*, she did complete successfully. She pulled several quilts into the living room and settled herself on the sofa with a bottle of water, some cheese she'd bought from her one trip to the store and two of the pastries from the Christmas Market.

She took a deep inhale and swore she could smell the lingering effects of Matteo's cologne. And there was nothing wrong with that. That smell, and the rain, and Italy – the mulled wine and earthy scents – would forever be instilled as the year she found herself with an Italian for Christmas.

As far as Chrstmas memories went it wasn't all that bad.

This certainly wasn't the Christmas Isabelle had grown up with and it definitely wasn't what she had in mind for this year, but with nothing to do and no schedule or demands, she found she was given an unexpected gift of time, which was precious in its own right.

And with a satisfied stomach, she snuggled into the sofa and watched the flames as they danced, deciding she was going to let herself dive deeper into the unexpected romance and simplicity of these days, and relish it all.

Chapter 13

I sabelle's phone yelled at her, screaming from where it had fallen in the middle of the night, under the coffee table. She blindly patted the floor and after locating it, brought it under the blankets where she'd burrowed to keep warm.

With one eye, she studied the time – ten thirty – and caller information before answering. "Hi mom. Are you on your way?" she muttered.

"How are you doing, honey? Are you holding up okay?"

"I'm okay," she yawned, "I slept in. I can't remember the last time I slept in this long."

"Are you sure you're okay?"

Isabelle opened her eyes and studied the darkened, back side of the sage green quilt. "I mean, I miss everyone and can't wait to see you, but we can't control the weather."

"No," her mother gave a frustrated sigh, "we can't."

"Uh oh." Isabelle knew that tone.

"We've been delayed *again*. Now they're saying we won't get out until Tuesday."

Tuesday was Christmas Eve.

"Well ..." What else could Isabelle say?

"Honey, I'm just so upset about this whole cluster *hmph*." Isabelle laughed, her mother had always replaced any intended foul language with sounds: hmphs, ems, ums ... "Izzy," she sighed.

"Mom, I know. This isn't how any of us wanted to spend the holiday. But look at it this way, you all have the perfect Christmas present for me. Showing up."

"Exactly. We'll be there soon and get this party started the right way."

"Okay." Isabelle pushed back the covers, was hit by the cold, and sank back into the cocoon. "Let me know when you're gonna get here and I'll meet you at the airport, then we'll get the vans and have a great week and a huge New Year party."

"Yes. Even if I have to force the *uh-uh* pilot to take off against their will, we'll be there soon!" She could hear her mother's definitive nod over the phone. "In the meantime … Izzy, you aren't waiting on us, are you? Have you been sightseeing, or done anything interesting?"

"Well …" Isabelle smiled to herself as she thought of all the *interesting* things she'd done. "I've seen a few sights. I saw the Duomo and went to a small hillside town and to the Christmas Market that smelled like spices and sugar."

"I can't wait, it sounds so decadent."

"You have no idea …"

"Okay, honey. Just … do you need to talk? What can I do?"

"Keep me posted, don't worry about me. It'll all work out."

"It'll all work out," her mom parroted.

Isabelle's phone began to beep that someone else was trying to call, and when she checked and saw Matteo's name, butterflies let loose, forcing a flush of heat to rush through her body. "Mom, I just woke up. I need to go to the bathroom."

"Okay, love you. Talk soon," she said and hung up.

Isabelle took a deep breath and let out a gleeful shake of her entire body before she calmly answered, "Buongiorno."

"Ah, buongiorno Isabella." *Good Lord, was his voice deeper over the phone?* "How are you?"

"Cold," she grinned, "how are you?"

"I am here."

"Where? Here, here?"

"Sì, a Casa Villa."

She sat up then, ignoring the wash of cold air as another flush followed to help warm her slightly.

Tangled in blankets, she tried to right herself, got caught and fell, just missing the coffee table and dropping her phone. Thankfully, all the quilts she took with her padded the fall.

"Isabella?" Matteo's muffled voice called through the phone.

She gave a laughing groan. "Just a second," she called out to the room.

She flopped about until finally freed from the quilts, then found the phone and crossed to a small mirror hanging in the living room. "I'm here, sorry, the phone fell." She brushed her hand through her hair, licked her finger to wipe away stray mascara under her eyes, then ran her tongue over her teeth.

"Isabella?" he called again.

"Give me one second." She hung up and made a large arc toward the door; first straightening her pajama pants and smoothing her shirt, she then grabbed the water bottle from the counter in the kitchen, swishing a drink around in her mouth before finally arriving at the door and swinging it open.

She pointed at him. "That's not fair." He was a fresh vision. Hair combed into place and cleanly shaved, which only accentuated his jaw and olive complexion (and she didn't know what she liked best, his shadowed beard and mussed hair, or this ... it was a toss-up as each held their own temptation). He wore black pants and another sweater, cream this time, a gray scarf and the camel colored coat (that she suddenly had plans to steal before they parted ways).

"What is not fair?" he asked.

She hugged the side of the door, not allowing him in, then gave a sigh; she wasn't done studying him yet. "You look so good. I just woke up and am a mess."

He held out a small wrapped package, maroon paper with gold lettering, a gold bow on top. "But I come with colazione."

"Co lots ee oh nay?" she repeated phonetically.

"Breakfast, brioche," he said, separating her away from the door with his free hand and slipping it around her waist, pulling her in close and brushing long, warm kisses on her cheeks.

She pressed herself into him and turned her head to accept his morning advances. "Fine, since you brought breakfast you can come in. I need help anyway."

"What do you need?"

"I'm freezing and the water heater wasn't working again last night."

He nodded, handed her the package, took off his coat and put it around her shoulders. "Where are the matches?"

After he lit the pilot light on the water heater, she waited until it was hot and then, like she'd done the first night together, left him for a shower.

When she got out, there was the unmistakable smell of a heater working and a roaring fire in the fireplace.

She nodded gratefully as she walked to the sofa. The quilts had been folded and stacked on a nearby chair and the small package was unwrapped, revealing four pastries on a gold paper tray.

"I bought so many pastries last night," she called to Matteo who was standing by the stove.

"These are fresh," he replied.

She watched him pour espresso into two small cups. When he brought them over, he offered her one before sitting next to her on the sofa.

"Thank you," she said as she inhaled the powerful elixir. "Thank you for the pastries and coffee and fixing the heat."

"I am sorry you had to spend another cold evening here."

She shrugged. "It's part of the adventure when you travel. How was your night? Did you get your perp?"

"Perp?"

"Perpetrator. The bad guy."

He pursed his lips. "Unfortunately, no."

She reached for one of the pastries, took a bite and rolled her eyes, shaking the scrumptious item at him. "You continue to ply me with coffee and pastries and Italian delicacies and Christmas lights and ..." His entertained gaze narrowed and a slight smile grew on his full lips – suddenly, finishing the sentiment that if he continued to ply her with such goods she would be his, felt very loaded.

"And?" he whispered.

"Don't you want one?" she asked.

He nodded and smoothly brushed a kiss on her lips, licking off the lingering sugar.

When he pulled away, she glanced between his lips, still so close, so tempting, but so was the pastry. With a grin she took a bite of the pastry, closed her eyes and sighed.

"Oh," he sat back and rubbed his hand against his chest, "I cannot believe I lost to a pastry." He picked one up and took a bite. "But I can understand."

"So what are we doing today? Do you need to work?"

He wiggled his eyebrows as he finished his bite, then said, "It has been insisted that we go to lunch."

"Insisted?"

"Sara. She will either kidnap you herself, or I am to bring you to Sunday lunch with the family."

"At the house with that amazing view?"

He nodded.

"What do we need to bring?"

"I was thinking we could bring a few bottles of wine from here."

"Perfect, what time do we need to leave?"

He glanced at his watch. "Thirty minutes?"

"Enough time to finish these and maybe make out?" She made the offer with the second pastry she held up.

"Make out?"

She licked her lips as she aimed a Cheshire grin at him. "Matteo, I'm probably going to throw myself at you and use the next thirty minutes to try to make up for all the heat I lost last night."

He raised an eyebrow and gave a long, interested nod of his head at the idea. "I would be happy to help in any way I can."

Isabelle sat back and started another strange game of 'Chicken' as she slowed down her eating and drinking pace and kept her attention on the fire; while out of the corner of her eye, watched to see if her slow pace was antagonizing Matteo.

Of course, he didn't seem like he was in a hurry for anything. It was her own need that clapped her hands free of sugar, took the cup out of his hand, then swung herself into a position of straddling his lap, propping herself up with her hands on either side of his head.

"Yes?" he asked.

Smiling, she took a deep breath through her nose and softened all her features as she let out a sigh. That brought about the growl she was looking for; his hands ran up her thighs, around her back, until one hand was twisted in her hair, pulling her head down so she could meet his lips.

They picked up where they'd left off the evening before, blindly seeking and twisting themselves up in each other, allowing their newly formed passion to burn.

Chapter 14

It was the sixth text message from Sara that finally pulled them away from each other. "She is reminding me that we promised to attend and she is getting in her car right now if I don't answer."

"Does she know where I'm staying?"

"I think I accidentally told her," he muttered.

Somehow they separated and got ready to leave. Then after stopping at the open wine tasting room to purchase a few bottles of wine, Matteo called his sister, making Isabelle verify that they were in the car, on the way.

When they arrived, he parked in the same place he had the day before; and once again, put the car in park but didn't turn it off.

Isabelle was fascinated by this. Even if she understood what he might be feeling, it still intrigued and entertained her.

He sighed as he finally turned off the car and faced her. "You have a big family?"

She nodded.

He scrubbed his face. "So you know most of them are in that house because I was caught holding your hand."

Again she nodded, and even though her eyes were twinkling, she was trying to give him the space to work through his feelings.

"We just met, and even though I *have* had a few relationships throughout the years, I have never brought any of them home."

She squeezed his forearm, an attempt to buoy him. "We're just friends. Who find each other attractive. And met in a delightfully unusual circumstance. And who are keeping each other warm while we're on Christmas vacation."

He scoffed, "Isabella, no matter what you say, do not tell my family that you will soon be going to Roma to work."

She raised an eyebrow at the request.

"Per favore," he drew out as he leaned across the center console toward her, "I got you released from jail, you owe me."

"I don't think the office I was waiting in was really a 'jail' ..."

"Isabella–" They were interrupted by a series of knocks on the passenger side window.

Three innocent looking dark-haired girls, all under eight years of age, were calling, "Zio!" in unison and giggling.

"Oh, they're sending the kids to do their dirty work." Isabelle laughed, having employed her own nieces and nephews in the same way throughout the years. She grinned as she opened the door. "Hi. Ciao," she called happily.

Matteo was walking around the car just as two of his nieces stood on either side of Isabelle, took her hands and began to drag her down the incline that would lead to the house.

And something about being taken by the hand and led into a home where several generations had lived, perched on the side of a hill overlooking the valley where the ancient city of Florence lay, propelled Isabelle into the most laid-back time warp there ever was.

Everything happened at the speed of light as she was embraced and kissed on the cheek and handed prosecco and wine and food while being gestured to a seat at the table, which yesterday had looked lonely. Now a leaf had been added and it was surrounded by conversation and laughter, warmth and heavenly smells of food. She heard music that might have been someone playing guitar in the other room or could just be the radio.

She was never directly asked what it was between her and Matteo. Though his siblings and extended family — which had become a jumble of names and connections she'd forgotten mere seconds after the introduction — were *very* happy to antagonize Matteo. (Of course, his nickname Babbeo was used more than his given name.)

Isabelle was happy to be brought into the fold of another family. It didn't increase her own loneliness, but actually brought about an excitement; the anticipation that soon the large rented villa would be filled with this kind of laughter and movement.

Kids continually brought her pictures and precious toys to show off and Isabelle cooed over their treasures. Matteo's sister Sara sat on her right, helping to translate throughout the day, while Matteo sat on her left.

In a raucous blink of an eye, several hours passed and Isabelle was sated by all the food and wine, and grateful for the overflowing kindness of strangers.

She had been captivated by the various moments when Matteo mindlessly rubbed her knee under the table, glanced longingly at her, and even the way he rested his arm across the back of her chair had excited her.

As the sun was setting, several visiting neighbors took their leave and Matteo was asked to help one of his older uncles out to his car. The kids were playing in the other rooms and the conversation had softened among the few people still lingering at the table.

Sara softly told Isabelle, "He really likes you."

"I like him too. But it's so unexpected," Isabelle admitted quietly.

A few things had happened in the past few hours. Not huge shifts, but interesting insights came to light in Isabelle's own life. She had some trepidation about moving to Rome for work for a year. But now, there was excitement that she would be able to continue to explore the passion of the people and culture.

Meeting someone that she was attracted to on her first day in the country was so unexpected. And the fact that he also worked in Rome, well, maybe it was a gift. And why not? People the world over built entire lifetimes on moments of unexpected coincidences.

"Unexpected is good," Sara said thoughtfully as she watched her brother return, waylaid by their father. "I think Matteo is the kind of man who has to be hit upside the head by a thing in order to see it."

The comment, along with Isabelle's relaxed bones, caused her to laugh aloud. "Well, that's exactly what I did to get his attention."

"You hit him?" Sara asked amused.

"Not *him*. I hit a sign post in front of him. To get his attention." She laughed at her joke and Sara nodded once as if she had just proved her point.

"Sara, I'm moving to Rome for the year for work," she said, biting her lower lip. She never really 'promised' Matteo she wouldn't tell anyone.

Sara's eyes widened and she glanced around the room, as if she were trying to decide if she was going to keep the information to herself, announce it to the room, or hold it for later.

Isabelle laughed and Sara let out a breath. "I won't tell anyone until after Christmas."

"That's in three days."

Sara laughed full-bodied, her short dark hair bouncing. "It will be the longest I've kept a secret. And it will be something amusing to just accidentally say in front of the family. To make Babbeo blush."

"Isabella?" Matteo reached her chair where he squatted down next to her so he could be at her eye level. "Can I take you for that after-dinner drink now?"

"The one we keep putting off?"

He nodded and she agreed.

If she had to guess, Isabelle would say it took another hour for them to break free from the house. Another whirlwind of embraces (with cheek pinches this time), more kisses and declarations of how nice it was to meet her were given. Then Matteo's mother handed over gifts of canned olives, homemade sausage and cheese. And Isabelle happily, if not greedily, accepted them.

They were once again in the car and Matteo let his head fall back against the headrest.

"Your family is wonderful."

"To you," he said, letting his head fall to the side so he could make eye contact.

"You got a lot of ribbing today, huh?"

"Ribbing?"

"Teasing," she amended.

He winked. "It was worth it."

She hugged her bag of goods to her chest. "It was, I have some very wonderful gifts here."

Matteo softly said, "Thank you."

"For what? I should be thanking you. I'd be all alone in a cold villa feeling sorry for myself if it wasn't for you."

He shook his head. "You aren't the kind of woman who feels sorry for herself."

"I'm not?"

He started the car. "You are the kind of woman who takes action when it's needed and is sensible enough to embrace the joys and hardships of this life. You are strong and funny and kind." He shrugged as he pulled away and Isabelle was elated at being seen that way by him, but he wasn't done with his compliments. "And, Isabella, you are very sexy."

Well, who was she to argue ...

Chapter 15

Once again, as they drove back into the city, traffic multiplied. She thought Matteo must be trying to make better time by using back streets; but then, most streets she'd been on in the past few days could have been categorized that way.

The current 'back street' however, well, she wasn't even sure it was meant for vehicles.

"Are we allowed to drive down here?" Isabelle asked, pulling the car door handle toward her as she leaned her body toward Matteo.

"Why wouldn't we be allowed to drive down here?" He swerved slightly to avoid a pothole and Isabelle sucked in a breath; when he didn't scrape against the walls of the buildings that seemed to be edging toward the car, or jump the curb, she let it out. "Because even in this small car I feel like we're about to hit the side of the walls."

"Eh, there is plenty of space." The car helped prove *her* point though when the tires slid against the curb slightly. She pulled harder on the door and sucked in her stomach while pressing her imaginary break.

Matteo mindlessly patted her knee. "We're almost there."

As he rolled to a stop at the end of the street, left blinker on, somehow missing the lineup of bikes sardined and chained together on unseen bike racks; she tried to focus on the dilapidated, yellow stucco wall plastered with weathered, curling posters promoting singers, bands and plays, rather than the lack of space.

Thankfully, the next street was wider, and soon they were pulling into an empty parking spot, a bit of luck it would seem, as every other spot was taken.

Turning the car off, he said, "Eccoci."

"Echo chee," she repeated and proceeded to peel her hand off the door handle.

"That means we are here."

"Eccoci," she muttered as she climbed out and shook off another eventful ride; once again wondering which sibling was going to weather the traffic with the oversized vans in an attempt to get everyone downtown to see all the sights.

As she studied the abandoned covered area and the rundown looking building behind it, Matteo read her mind and explained, "This is the Mercato Sant'Ambrogio. Under these covered areas they sell seasonal fruits and vegetables. Inside, is a very large area with permanent stalls where meats and salamis and cheese are sold. But they close in the early afternoon." He waved to the building then took her hand and brought it to his lips to brush a kiss against it, then declared, "Oh! You should bring your family here. They also have fresh pasta and olive oils ..." He glanced around and pointed to the covered area farthest from them. "And I think that is where they set up the antique market."

As she studied the empty space she asked, "Is it like the Christmas Market?"

"A little, there are many vendors and different things for sale. Fish, pastries, nuts ..." he gave a wave of his hand, "your family will enjoy it. This is where the locals shop."

Leaving the market behind, they meandered through the streets until the path they were on brought them to a small piazza where six streets intersected.

While most businesses were closed, two restaurants and a pharmacy were busy with the comings and goings of customers.

They bypassed the restaurants, their destination a cafe across the piazza where several tables were set up outside, surrounded by heat lamps.

Of course, lights were strung above the small expanse of the piazza, painting the cobblestone a glittering gray.

The surrounding five-story buildings dwarfed the simple beige facade of an apparent church – massive wooden double doors were topped with a faded fresco of Mary holding her baby, while long forgotten saints by her side looked on.

Two young men sat on the top steps leading to the church, playing guitars; a soft jazzy number that echoed off the buildings.

Matteo led them to an empty outside table near a heat lamp that did a fabulous job fighting off the cold, giving them a perfect view of the piazza so they could people-watch. He gestured for her to sit, then repositioned the other chair so he could sit next to her as he explained, "This is a nice place to have a digestivo."

"Dee-jest-ivo," she repeated. "The after dinner drink you promised me the other night?"

He shrugged. "Or maybe you would like something to eat instead?"

"I don't think I could fit anything else." Isabelle sat back and protruded her stomach through her jacket. "Your mom kept bringing food. She was sitting at the table, so I know she wasn't cooking all day, but every time she got up she brought more food. Where was it coming from?"

He winked as he lounged back and draped his arm around her chair. "Italian mammas are magic."

"That is the only reasonable explanation."

When the waiter came to take their orders, Isabelle shrugged and asked Matteo to order her something Italian.

The waiter returned shortly with the Italian version of mulled wine. "This is called a Vin Brulé," Matteo explained.

She took an appreciative sip of the comforting, richly spiced wine and nodded happily. "*This* is exactly what I didn't know I wanted."

Matteo slipped his arm from the chair to her waist, then dipped his head to her neck, nuzzling through her scarf to make contact with flesh. Isabelle laughed and worried that her reaction was what caused him to pause. She was about to apologize, but his hold on her changed to something a bit more possessive than playful.

"Isabella," the whisper of her name had a wary tone, "you are never going to believe this."

She ran through the things she wouldn't believe and went with, "You're calling me another cab because you have to work?"

He slowly straightened and when she glanced at him, realized he wasn't looking at her but behind her back, across the piazza.

"What?" She followed his gaze.

He shook his head as he said, "That pickpocket we are looking for ..."

"Is he here?"

He gave a *humph* of disbelief followed by a description. "The man in the green jacket."

She watched the man linger near a group of people as he easily, so smoothly, bumped into one of the men, then walking away, slipped something into his own pocket.

"Matteo," she whispered, incredulous.

"I'm sorry," he said and she dislodged herself from him and pushed gently on his chest, quietly demanding, "You gotta go."

His attention fluctuated between Isabelle and the man. "I'll be–"

"Go," she whispered intently, nodding at the piazza with big eyes, worried that yelling for Matteo to go would bring unwanted attention.

"Just ... wait here."

She nodded her head emphatically in agreement but after two steps, Matteo retraced his path, grinned as he quickly kissed her, then left.

Slowly sauntering through the piazza, he made a wide berth. Isabelle brought her drink to her lips, eyes wide, slightly worried, but strangely a bit excited to watch the unfolding scene.

The pickpocket hit another unsuspecting person and Matteo caught the attention of two police officers who she hadn't even noticed at another side of the piazza; they'd been hovering in the shadows smoking, so she was sure the pickpocket hadn't noticed them either.

Matteo pulled something out of his pocket, probably his credentials. His hands and mouth moved quickly in explanation, but there were no sudden movements, just three men taking turns scanning the area.

When they finally separated and began walking in different directions, Isabelle could tell they were moving into positions meant to cut off the perpetrator's escape routes. She sat forward, clutching her glass. There wasn't any threat in the air, and it was fascinating to watch Matteo. He ambled really; unhurried and so calm. To be fair, the officers didn't seem to be worried either, she thought they looked more frustrated with the interruption of their smoke break than anything.

When they'd triangulated, they began to slowly encroach on the pickpocket, and just when Isabelle figured the man should know what was happening, but too late, he spotted the first officer; turning slowly he found the second one, which forced him directly into Matteo's path.

Matteo had the advantage, the pickpocket didn't know who he was, so when he lunged to begin running, Matteo was able to grab him by the arm and trip him at the same time, taking the man to the ground in a seamless move that caused a grunt to echo off the buildings and the crowd nearby to gasp.

Isabelle put her glass down and began clapping; receiving random raised eyebrows from the patrons surrounding her. She pointed to Matteo and they followed her finger, shrugging before going back to their conversations and meals.

"Well, *I* thought it was impressive," she muttered as the waiter arrived, checking on her to see if the clapping had been because she needed something.

She shook her head and sat back, letting out a sigh of relief. Matteo was capable enough. She'd been around enough law enforcement to know they were well-trained, and he would be too. But there was something about seeing the whole process unfold, and being (a little) emotionally attached to the man who was doing the takedown, added a slight element of concern that was quite different for her.

The police joined Matteo and once the man was cuffed and hauled to his feet, she knew Matteo was explaining he needed a moment. He all but swaggered over to her, a slight hitch to his eyebrow when he was close enough, silently asking if she'd seen that.

"Impressive," she commented.

He held out his hand for her, she took it and was glad when he pulled her against him and followed the motion by sealing his lips to hers. Her stomach punched and heat tingled throughout her body. She slipped her arms around his neck and held on tight, but all too soon he pulled away and she knew what was coming.

"Matteo, you are making quite the habit of getting me all heated up and then leaving."

"Bella–" he began but she put a finger to his lips. "I get it. I really do."

"I am sorry."

"I'll take a taxi."

"I'll arrange it."

This time, after Isabelle waved goodbye to another taxi driver and walked into the oversized, empty villa, it was at least warm.

Chapter 16

S omeone was knocking.

Isabelle tried to roll over on the sofa to keep herself adrift in a dream, pulling the quilt over her head to drown out the sound.

Her body relaxed into that sweet space between awake and sleep, again reaching for the shores of her dreams.

But the knock came again. And this time, the pounding was more demanding.

She forced her eyes open with a grunt; this time of year, when something is knocking in the middle of the night, it was bound to be the ghost of Christmas Past, Present or Future.

She blinked, trying to remember where she was just as her phone began to ring.

She patted around for the phone, and one open eye revealed it was Matteo. When she answered it with a muttered "hi" the knocking on the door stopped.

"Isabella, I am here at the villa."

"You are? What time is it?"

"Four in the morning."

She yawned and mumbled, "givemeasec" as she tried to convince the layers of quilts to release her, then started to shuffle toward the front door, scrubbing her face as she went. When she was halfway down the hall, she couldn't recall where the light switch was, so turned back and found the switch for the kitchen. Then, in the glow that spilled, she shuffled back, stubbed her toes on the table by the front door, swore under her breath, and bleary-eyed, fumbled to open said door.

She was met by a blast of cold air and a shadowed Matteo. She waved him inside and before she could say anything, he excitedly stated, "You are a forensic anthropologist."

"I know."

"Do you believe in fate?" He laughed, which pulled a frown.

"What?"

"I need your help."

"Okay?"

"You said you have worked on police cases before, yes?"

It was too early for this line of questioning. "Matteo, what's going on?"

"I need help with my case."

"The pickpocket?"

"Yes."

She scrubbed her face again, then widened and blinked her eyes to wake herself up. "I'm confused."

He nodded. "Can you get ready and I'll explain everything to you on the way." He took her hand and pulled her toward the rooms.

"You haven't been to bed yet, have you?" It was more of a statement than a question.

"No." He stopped in the hallway and frowned, he didn't know which room she'd claimed as hers.

She pointed and he continued to walk and talk with her in tow. "There are normally two technicians in the lab here. That test DNA. Can you perform DNA testing?" He flipped on the overhead light in the room.

Isabelle squinted. "It depends on the lab and what needs to be done."

"I knew you could do it."

"Matteo, I don't know what you need done and I'm not sure how I'm going to help." She sighed.

He laughed again and gave her a sideways hug. "I am excited. And tired. Put some clothes on and we'll talk more in the car. Could you please bring your passport as well? For identification." He pulled the door shut after him.

They didn't immediately leave, as he had brewed a pot of espresso, poured two cups and was setting them on the table when she entered the kitchen with her jacket and purse over her arm.

"I thought you were in a hurry."

"There's always time for espresso."

"This country," she muttered, shaking her head as she stifled a yawn.

In the car, there was no sign of the coming dawn. Matteo apologized for his hasty appearance and excitement. He began the explanation he tried earlier, "The technicians at the lab are gone for the holiday. One has gone to Canada, and the other is in southern Italy. But it is very important to this case to have some bones tested for DNA. To see if they are a match."

"Okay. That actually sounds like something in my wheelhouse."

"Wheelhouse?"

"Something that has to do with the work I normally do."

"Yes. I think meeting you has been very ..." he frowned, "the word is fortuita in Italian."

"Fortuitous?" she offered.

"I think so." He blindly reached for her hand and gave it a squeeze. "Thank you for coming to help me."

"Don't get too excited. I don't know if I can help you yet or not."

They were back to the center of the city, only this early in the morning, there was no traffic. Isabelle pursed her lips as she watched the lit stucco and brick pass; maybe she could convince everyone to leave the house by six in the morning. Then driving might be a little less of an undertaking. "What time do most shops open in the morning downtown?"

"Probably nine or ten. Is there somewhere you would like to go?"

"No. I was just wondering."

He pulled into a parking garage then led her to the back of a three-store building. But the two officers who stood in front of the door, dressed in dark blue with tactical vests, black berets, and holding intimidating automatic weapons, stopped her in her tracks.

Matteo walked in front of her, showed the men his ID, then turned and gestured to Isabelle. After a moment he stepped back to her and asked, "Isabella, you brought your passport?"

She fumbled through her purse and handed the ID to Matteo. He in turn showed it to the men to scrutinize, and after a conversation done through their earpieces with an unseen person in charge, she was cleared to enter the building.

As the door closed behind them she whispered to Matteo, "What kind of pickpocket was this?"

They soon came to another guarded door; where the twins of the armed men from outside stood. And even though they didn't ask for ID, they still intimidated her.

Matteo held the door, and she relaxed as they entered the lab. *This* was what she knew: staging rooms, testing rooms, break rooms and clean labs. Inside, she was greeted by an older man (no gun, so that helped to calm her down further), who stood next to two large silver equipment cases. Thin and distinguished looking, he wore a stylish black suit, was clean shaven and without a single one of his thick dark hairs out of place; his well-rested demeanor was quite the contrast to her abruptly woken self. In the center of the room, on one of three stainless steel worktables, was a very large dirty green duffle bag that looked as if it'd once been buried.

"Isabella, this is Signor Conti," Matteo introduced. "He is the head curator of the Museo Galileo here in Firenze."

She offered her hand and he shook it with a slight incline of his head.

"He is here to supervise. To make sure no harm comes to anything."

"No harm comes to anything ..." Isabelle repeated as she glanced between the men, the duffle bag and the two large cases.

"Isabella, I have been working to track down a man of interest, and the pickpocket I arrested this evening, he was working for this man. It is a very long story, but I believe the bag I liberated using the information I was given, is very important." He put on a pair of latex gloves and unzipped the bag, gesturing for Isabelle to join him. She watched as he pulled out a bubble wrapped item, and wasn't too shocked when he revealed a femur.

"We think these are the bones of Galileo," Matteo said excitedly.

Now *that*, was a shock.

"What?"

"Now you understand why testing them cannot wait."

"How are you going to test them?" she asked.

"*You* are going to test them," Matteo explained, as if Isabelle wasn't following.

"How? What do you mean Galileo? Like, *the* Galileo?"

"Sì."

"But ... you said DNA testing."

"Yes, I did."

"Do people in Italy just happen to have Galileo's DNA on file?"

"Yes. In a way."

"What?" She felt like she was in a fever dream. She pointed to the man standing stoically nearby. "Is he like ... are you a known relative or something?"

Galileo?!

"No." Matteo said something to Signore Conti, who nodded, then opened the first case, and with great care and efficiency, freed its contents. His reverence for the large glass egg he took out spoke volumes. The glass-shaped egg was mounted on a brass pedestal and had a matching brass lattice work around the center, so the egg could be opened. But really, none of the detailing about the egg was important when Isabelle realized what was held within it – the bones of a human finger.

"A finger?" she said aloud, more to hear herself speak.

The grin could be heard in Matteo's voice as he corrected her, "*Galileo's* finger."

"What?!"

Chapter 17

I sabelle rubbed her eyes and took a deep breath. Then, when she could focus, took a step toward the digit in the glass egg and frowned as she studied it. "*This* is Galileo's finger. How do you know?"

Signor Conti, who up until this moment had only spoken in Italian, responded in English, "How much do you know about Galileo?"

She gave a slight shake of her head. "He made strides in astronomy and math. He was the first one to say that Earth orbits the Sun and was ... killed for it?" A shrug of her shoulders. "It's been a while. I don't know a lot about him."

The man gave an understanding nod. "Not everyone spends their entire careers dedicated to studying and keeping the memory of the man alive. He was indeed considered il padre dell'astronomiathe, the father of math and astronomy. He had many other discoveries also and he did declare the Earth orbits the Sun. But he was not put to death for this. Instead, he was judged in a trial in 1633 by the Roman Inquisition for eresia, heresy. They found him guilty and he was condemned to live in his home for the remainder of his life."

"House arrest?" Isabelle asked.

The man nodded. "He died when he was seventy-seven years old of a heart attack that was, perhaps, brought on by a fever he had."

"Why did I think he was younger when he died? How old was he when he was put on trial?"

"Seventy years of age," the curator answered before continuing his original storyline, "So because he was a heretic, he was not allowed to be buried in a Catholic manner. However, in the year 1737, the church realized he had spoken the truth and he was forgiven. His bones were taken from an unconsecrated box underneath the bell tower in Santa Croce and moved to a tomb inside the church. There was a large ceremony and many important people attended. Among them were a famous botanist, anatomist, antiquarian and marquis. They removed Galileo's thumb, index finger, middle finger, along with one tooth and his fifth lumbar vertebra."

Isabelle's eyes widened as the list of 'taken' bones grew. "So ..." She wasn't sure what question she had.

"You want to know why they took the bones," Signor Conti supplied; she nodded her affirmation. "The man who took them said he *had* to do it, because Galileo wrote so many beautiful things with those fingers."

Isabelle shook her head in wonder as questions swirled, but she kept them to herself to let the curator continue.

"The vertebra was donated to the University of Padua and we only had one finger. The rest were thought to be lost to time. Until several years ago, when our director was contacted by a man who purchased some unidentified artifacts at an auction. Among them were a thumb, index finger and tooth. They were donated to the museum when they were verified."

He walked over to the duffle bag. "Allora, signora, if you would take out the bones and place them just here."

She glanced at Matteo. "I'm assuming it's just the three of us because this needs to be handled very quietly?"

He winked at her.

"Do you need photographs?" she asked.

"The bag has been photographed, including a view of it unzipped. I and Signor Conti are here to verify the handling of the bones."

She nodded. "Okay. I need to see what tools the lab has and then I think we all need to put on protective clothing to prevent further contamination ..."

He gestured across the room to where several sterile suits were hanging.

It was surreal what Matteo was asking of her. She could do a rapid DNA test, but that was something she did when there was ample bone matrix to release the DNA.

These bones were old; the finger, now mocking her, was brittle. What happened if she took a sample and it crumbled to dust? The police were already wanting to throw her in jail and kick her out of Florence for accidentally falling in a fountain. What would happen to her if she ruined an honest to god relic?

After they were properly attired, she stood in front of the bag and tried to steady her breathing.

"Bella?" Matteo called.

She muttered, "Give me a second," as she flexed her hands to stop the unexpected shaking brought about by the unanticipated task set before her.

"Are you alright?"

She shook her head. "It isn't every day you're woken up before the sun and asked to test bones that may or may not belong to *the* Galileo."

"Ah, then take a few moments."

A few moments. She took a deep breath and blew it out, finally taking out the first bubble wrapped bone, carefully unwrapping it and following it with another and another. Until she finally had a decent amount of bones laid out before her. They were significantly weathered, a white grayish color.

"The bones are brittle, showing signs of mineralization where the organic material has decomposed, leaving behind a primary calcium-based structure." She gave the description, as if she were beginning a project and going through the logical steps; the description and first impressions were always what she recorded first. And going through the usual actions calmed her nerves. "Consistent with rather old remains."

As she carefully arranged the bones, she continued, "They are in pretty good shape for being wrapped and mishandled. No overwhelming signs of erosion or damage from environmental factors."

When she found the skull, she turned it gently, nodding and pointing to a line that ran the length of the skull. "See this squiggly line? It's completely fused. That means this person was over forty years old. It fuses fully by age forty."

The curator stepped closer to study the skull, then pointed at the lower jaw. "There are no teeth remaining, this verifies the stories. The reason the tooth was taken was because it was the only tooth remaining in the lower jaw."

"So Florentine dentistry wasn't high on the scientific spectrum?" Her joke fell flat.

She continued to liberate the rest of the bones, pausing to study a rib. "See how the ends are thin and have sharp edges? That's something else you find in older adults."

She was quiet as she continued, becoming lost in her work. It wasn't until she had everything arranged that she turned her attention back to the bones of the right wrist and hand, shaking her head as she lightly touched them. "The thumb, index finger and middle finger are missing."

She felt a wave of dizziness wash over her. Excitement, trepidation, disbelief? It was probably a mixture of them all. "They were well-organized and preserved. For being in a duffle bag."

She straightened her shoulders and looked across at Matteo. "There are several ways to go about this, and I'm assuming that time is pretty important?"

Matteo nodded.

She bit her lip as her gaze drifted between the recreated skeleton and the finger in the glass egg. "In that case, we'd normally perform a rapid bone test. And this lab is set up for it ..." She turned slowly in a circle.

"How long does that take?" Matteo asked.

"About twelve hours ... but that's when the bone matrix can fully release the DNA." She cleared her throat. "I'm assuming we're not allowed to dissolve Galileo's bones."

"Please, do not do that." The curator quickly verified her assumption.

"Then ... I think the best way to go about it is to do some scrapings and use that material and see what results we can get."

"Perfect." Matteo clapped his hands together, but she tilted her head to the side, saying, "Matteo, I can't promise this'll show much. These are old bones. We do a lot more work to get conclusive tests, and normally, those take about four months or longer."

He nodded. "We just need to know if there is a *possibility*."

"Okay, then let's see about this possibility. But if we do find some matching markers ..."

Matteo shrugged, confirming her suspicions, "There will be some quick intervention and several agencies involved and months of testing."

"Then I suppose ... here we go." She said the words to propel herself into action, but it wasn't working.

Matteo stepped closer and elbowed her. "Isabella, is this not how you imagined you would be spending your Christmas?"

She gave an unladylike snort. "This is *so* far from how I imagined things would be going. I didn't even have Galileo's museum on the list of things to see and do." She glanced at the curator. "No offense."

He offered a slight incline of his head, affirming he wasn't offended. "Perhaps now, you might like to come see us? I can arrange for a private tour for you and your family."

She was going to have one hell of a story to share. (That was, if she were allowed to. Red tape and intelligence communities might mean she would have to stay tight-lipped for a while.) "That would be wonderful, thank you."

Impressed by the organization and proficiency of the lab, she began to pull out the equipment and solutions she was going to need. "If this is Galileo ... I thought you said he was buried in ..."

"Santa Croce," Signor Conti offered.

"Then how ..."

"That's what we're trying to figure out," Matteo said. "There are several theories still. But the man I arrested–"

"The pickpocket?"

"Yes. He is what you would call a low-level worker for a more important person. And as I thought, our little pickpocket knew of another man who had this bag in his possession and was acting as the transporter. So there are still people following that trail, but my job now is to stay with this matter."

"If this is a match, will they excavate the tomb in the church?"

"Perhaps." The curator shrugged. "We are so very far from such a thing."

"Okay then." Isabelle stretched her head to the right and left and clapped her hands together. "I'm going to need help from both of you."

Chapter 18

Isabelle paced the length of the small break room and on her third lap, Matteo appeared with a brown paper bag, holding it from the bottom. "Are you sure you don't want me to take you back to the villa? Or my family's home? You can get some rest." He'd made the offer several times now.

"Are you gonna go rest?"

He shot her a smile and shook his head.

"Then don't you dare offer to separate me from Galileo's bones." She chuckled and admitted, "I'm too excited and enthralled. And ... eager. And other words that start with 'e'." She pointed to the bag he was carrying. "So let's eat."

He hoisted the bag slightly into the air in agreement.

Isabelle stood next to him as he pulled out a sandwich wrapped in white paper with red writing, and handed it over. She was already taking a second bite when he listed the ingredients, "That panini has mortadella, ricotta cheese and fresh tomato."

With a full mouth she said, "It's amazing. I didn't realize how hungry I was."

He pulled out four more sandwiches. She nodded to them, a silent inquiry as to who they belonged to.

"I didn't know what kind you might like, so I purchased a few. And one for Signor Conti."

She took another bite then pointed it slightly in Matteo's direction. "This is good and I'll definitely take another one."

He handed another one over. "I think you'll like this one. It has Scamorza, a popular cheese, with grilled zucchini and pistachio cream."

She grinned, abandoning the one she'd eaten half of to take the new offer. The first bite was eye-rolling good; she waved the sandwich at Matteo to verbalize her feelings. "So good."

Another few bites and she sat down and sighed, arranging the bottle of water she'd found in the break room and the rest of her sandwiches.

"I'll go tell Signor Conti he can come eat as soon as I'm done," she said.

They decided that no one would leave the bones or lab alone. Even though it was guarded. All three talked about how they felt this was of the utmost importance. Signor Conti believed the entire reputation of the Galileo Museum and the research connected to the institute was at stake.

Matteo's reasons were work related. And for Isabelle, it was the pure excitement that pumped adrenaline through her veins as 'what if' storylines bumped around in her head.

Even if the bones didn't belong to Galileo, they were still old and found in Italy; an extension of the work she would be starting in the new year.

"Matteo, I don't know if I've ever been so excited by a project I've worked on," she confessed.

He raised an eyebrow. "Really? I find that hard to believe. I think you are one of those people who is very good at their job because they love it."

"I do. I really do." Most of the time it felt like she was playing at work. She had an unsubstantiated fear that someone might find out and a Secret Society of the Miserable would be employed to take it all away from her.

But she loved her job, the puzzle and stories of the past she was able to tangibly piece back together. The opportunities to travel and work all over the world. It often seemed like a dream.

"I think you like your job as well," she said.

"How do you know?"

"You get a certain kind of ... confidence when you're talking about it or in the middle of a case. There's a swagger about you."

"Swagger?"

"You know who you are, what you're about and you're comfortable with it."

"Am I?" He leaned forward as she talked, rather enjoying her compliments.

She swatted playfully at his arm. "You know what I'm saying is true."

"Forse." He winked. "I am still not sure what to make of the coincidence of meeting you."

"Fate and destiny? They aren't scientific ideas, but philosophical ones. What did the men of the Renaissance think?"

"I think those men are still debating it after all this time," Matteo offered.

Isabelle liked that idea. She went back to her original thought. "I've handled some extraordinary specimens over the years, but you have to admit, this is pretty spectacular."

"I admit it." He took a bite of his sandwich and sat back as he thoughtfully chewed.

Isabelle studied his relaxed, unpulsed posture. "Does anything upset you? Other than your family?"

He shrugged. "I've learned through my job and life that worrying and getting upset will waste a lot of energy. I anticipate and plan for different outcomes. But my family, it's different because they know exactly how to antagonizzare, antagonize me."

She thought of her older brothers who continued to delight in antagonizing her. "Yeah, but we know how to push them back."

He wiggled his eyebrows in reply.

They drifted through their own thoughts as they finished eating. When they were done, they went to relieve the curator.

"What does it mean if the bones do belong to Galielo?" Isabelle asked.

"That you were allowed to work with Galileo," he teased but the answer sent shivers throughout her body; *that* was one of the most striking takeaways. "It means either Santa Croce was looted, right under their own noses, or Galileo was never reburied. Or, a hundred more theories will need to be looked at."

She shook her head to dislodge the dreamy, unreal effect the day was having. "You know, this whole week has been far from what I had planned."

"For me also."

"But in a good way?" She sought the compliment.

He pulled her to his side and his voice lowered as he confirmed, "In the best way."

The next hours were spent pacing and talking. After the curator ate, he began to weave the story of Galileo's life. How the man never married, but for a time lived with a woman who gave birth to three of his children. Two girls and a boy.

Signor Conti talked animatedly about Galileo's scientific inventions, mathematical findings, and theories. He pulled out his phone and showed off photos of several inventions housed in the museum. But when he scrolled past six sketches of the Moon, Isabelle stopped him.

"Ah, the *Sidereus Nuncius*. Galileo wrote a pamphlet, the astronomical treatise that holds drawings and diagrams of the Moon and certain constellations." He zoomed in on one of the sketches. "At that time, most scientists believed the Moon was smooth. Galileo discovered it was not so. He explained that the Moon has mountains and valleys. Just like Earth."

She shot a smile at Matteo standing on the other side of the curator.

The photo was swiped away, replaced by a picture of the finger in the glass egg displayed in its case.

"Signora Miller. Do you know why the finger was kept in the position, pointing up?" he asked.

Isabelle shook her head; it was strange enough that there was a finger in a glass egg, so the fact that there might be a reason for its positioning had been lost on her.

"It is pointing to the sky; a reminder for those who view it, to continue gazing up. To reach for the stars. Philosophically and realistically."

They all three jumped when the timer indicating the test was over, went off.

Isabelle's hands shook as she pushed several buttons on the machine that would print out the results. To calm herself she pointed out the obvious, "I'm printing the results so we can analyze them."

She stood at the printer for quite a while, Matteo looking over her right shoulder, Signor Conti over the left.

"What does it mean?" Matteo asked after a moment.

Her hands were physically shaking as she turned an astonished grin to Matteo and hoarsely whispered, "There is a profile match."

He clapped his hands and pulled her into his arms to brush a kiss on her forehead. Isabelle kept a tight hold on the papers to steady herself and out of the corner of her eye, she watched the curator sag against the counter.

The moment hung in the air, stealing the breath and life from it; waiting until Isabelle exhaled.

Matteo pulled his phone out just as the curator did the same. Both men began talking quickly and frantically to whomever answered their respective calls.

Isabelle shuffled over to the bones and laid her hand on the top of the skull. "Galileo," she whispered. And as if she needed to be pinched to make sure she was awake, she repeated his name, "Galileo, sir. I'm Isabelle Miller. We're going to take good care of you now."

She had a feeling there was going to be a lot of action in this lab very soon.

And there was.

After hours of just the three of them waiting in the cool, sterile building, the room at last began to fill with official looking men and women; some she figured were in various intelligence fields. She was quickly introduced to the mayor and the superintendency of Archaeology, who looked like he was going to be sick.

Isabelle was asked question after question; Matteo helped with translation and once her information had been recorded and she'd signed a non-disclosure form, she was dismissed.

Matteo however, was far from done.

"I'll walk you out," he said.

They were quiet as they retraced their steps, and when they turned a corner to an empty hall, Isabelle tugged on Matteo's arm to stop him; it was all the encouragement he needed to press her against the nearest wall and devour her lips with his own.

The climax of the day, the overwhelming find – their excitement overflowed, spilling out of them. Isabelle's hands were desperate as she tried to find part of Matteo to hold onto and explore more at the same time. When she slid her hands under his shirt and they came in contact with hard flesh, she wasn't sure who moaned louder. Matteo's hands multiplied and when they too came in contact with the skin on her back, slipping around to the front to cup her breasts, she felt animalistic urges take over and wondered if they could find an unlocked office to fall into.

Instead, as with every other moment that grew in temperature and need between them, they were interrupted.

A deep voice, calling "Arcuri" and clearing his throat, pulled them apart. Matteo glanced over his shoulder and upon seeing the owner, helped right Isabelle before himself.

"Isabella, this is the deputy director of the External Intelligence and Security Agency."

He then spoke to the director in Italian, appearing to continue the introduction. Isabelle tried not to blush as she shook the man's hand and Matteo explained, "I told him you are the one who tested the bones for us."

The man gave a gruff "grazie" to Isabelle followed by an unspoken eyebrow raise that meant it was time for Matteo to get back to work.

"There is a car waiting to take you back to the Casa Villa. Will you be okay?"

"Yes. How long ...?" She waved the question away. "You don't know how long you'll be. Call me if you get a chance. I'm going to try and get some sleep."

"Will you be able to sleep?"

She gave an incredulous laugh. "I just proved a bag of stolen bones belonged to Galileo. I don't think so."

Chapter 19

B y the time Isabelle was delivered back to the villa it was eight in the evening. She took a shower, made a fire and poured the last glass of wine from the bottle she and Matteo had shared just two days ago.

She replayed the testing she'd done. As she stared into the flickering flames of the fire, she went through the entire process; not because she'd done something wrong, but to mentally double-check her work.

It was sound. She was meticulous and knowing that her work would be questioned, she made sure to write down each step she took and asked Matteo to take photographs throughout the process. Even though he said there was no need. Now she was glad she had.

"Galileo," she whispered. Would she have any more contact with the father of astronomy before she continued to Rome? From the motley group that showed up and the phone calls being made, she had a feeling the answer to that question was no.

Would she ever work with Matteo again?

That was an interesting thought that stirred to life at the same moment a snap of dry wood released a shower of crackling sparks.

He hadn't lied to her when he told her he worked for an 'intelligence agency,' but the nonchalant way he'd talked about it and the fact that he was looking for a pickpocket as part of his job, had all alluded to it being a more subdued part of law enforcement. But from the intimidating ranking of the people she'd been introduced to in the past few hours, it would seem his job was more than he'd let on.

What did that mean for Isabelle, though?

His job might be a bit more dangerous, but there was no fear attached to the idea. She knew, like a sixth sense, he was capable and careful.

The day had peeled back more layers of personality for both of them.

And that kiss ... why did it seem that the moment each of their kisses reached a peak, at the moment of combustion, they'd been doused. Her desperation to be alone with him and finally free to explore the rhythms they could create was becoming a hunger, and there was only one way to satisfy that yearning.

The next time he came knocking, she wasn't going anywhere with him until they finally followed those burning kisses to their satisfied, exhausted end.

She shivered as the past few days – unexpected, lovely, life-changing days – brushed past her. This was definitely a holiday season she'd never forget.

Isabelle blinked her eyes open. Something had woken her. She lay still, and her eyes were beginning to slip closed again when she heard a knocking.

She grinned, her previous evening's thoughts hurrying her off the sofa.

The quilts tried to trip her again, but she kept upright this time and did a twirl then fluttered her fingers in triumph at them.

"Coming!" she yelled at the door.

She swung the door open with a wide grin pasted to her face, but it wasn't Matteo standing on the other side.

Though it was just as much of a shock.

"Buongiorno." Sara beamed.

"Morning." Isabelle crossed her arms over her braless shirt. "What are you doing here? Not that you aren't welcome ... I just ... what's going on?"

Sara wiggled her eyebrows and stepped aside; her husband and children were climbing out of a car that had a Christmas tree tied to the roof.

"Matteo told me your parents are on their way and you do not have a tree. He also told me that you might be running low on groceries." She held up her hands, a yellow plastic bag in each one.

"Oh, Sara. You didn't have to do that. I was planning on going to town today to get a few things."

"Now you do not have to." Sara pushed past Isabelle and as she made her way to the kitchen, called out, "This is lovely."

"I think so," Isabelle muttered, watching Sara pull out packages of meats, cheeses, a loaf of bread, a bottle of wine, some fresh pasta and two jars of sauce.

A whirlwind of children came arguing into the kitchen, each carrying another bag. These Sara directed to the living room. "We bought a few ornaments for the tree also."

Isabelle's phone began to ring, so she went to retrieve it and seeing Matteo's name, regained some of her earlier excitement.

"Hello?"

"My sister is on her way and I couldn't stop her," he said immediately.

"She's already here."

"Mi dispiace. I'm sorry."

"Don't be. It's a wonderful surprise."

"What is a wonderful surprise?"

"Her family is here, they brought groceries and a tree."

"She said she was just going to take you breakfast, and she was going alone," he said in exasperation.

"Where are you?" Isabelle asked the question she *really* wanted the answer to.

"I'm still at the lab."

"How long have you been awake?" she asked, concerned.

"I was able to rest for a few hours last night." He changed the subject. "Have you heard from your parents?"

"Not yet."

"Tonight is Christmas Eve. My family usually goes to Midnight Mass at the Duomo. I don't know if that sounds like something you would like to do or–"

"Yes," Isabelle answered.

"I am not sure when I will be able to leave here. But I want to try to get a little sleep and then I can pick you up."

"I have pasta and sauce and a new bottle of wine," she offered. "If you wanted to sleep here …"

He groaned and the sound floated from a three-story lab in the center of Florence, around the curvy Tuscan roads and into the Casa Villa to heat every part of her body.

"Bella, I will see what I can do. Don't let my sister be too bossy."

"I won't."

"And I'll let you know when I am on my way."

She hung up and when she turned around found Sara, her husband, and their three kids grinning at her.

"I like him, okay," she defended.

"I know." Sara swatted the air in front of her to dismiss the topic. "Where should we put the tree?"

Chapter 20

The day got away from Isabelle.

Sara cooked a veggie frittata for everyone while her husband, Luca, righted the tree in the corner of the living room and their children – Aldo, Elena and Chiara – happily began a lopsided decoration.

Isabelle's brother called, the family was at the airport and the flight was still scheduled to leave on time. Chances were very good they would make it late, but in time for some of Christmas Day.

Feeling lighter, Isabelle relaxed into the company of the unannounced visitors. They took a long walk through the vineyard and enjoyed a wine tasting at the estate.

When Matteo called and updated her on his progress – he would be later than intended and needed to change clothes – Sara, making sure she could overhear the conversation, offered a solution. She would bring Isabelle to their parents' home. Since everyone who was going to the Duomo for Midnight Mass was meeting there first anyway to eat, it was the perfect solution.

Matteo apologized to Isabelle but she was looking forward to spending more time with his family. They were lively and welcoming. And the promise of eating more of his mother's food was a motivating temptation.

This time, however, Isabelle drove her own car. (There wasn't room with Sara's family.) When Sara volunteered to drive Isabelle, Luca suggested Isabelle could manage on her own. And she did. Either she was getting used to the traffic, or she'd found a little more confidence because the drive didn't feel as horrifying as the first one had been.

She was welcomed into the Arcuri household once more with hugs, and plied with food.

She'd been propped up at the dinner table with photo albums and stories. Sara sat next to her once again, while one of the small nephews was coloring on her other side. She had thrown her head back in laughter at the story she was being told, and it was when her gaze focused once more that she found an exhausted Matteo leaning against the doorway of the dining room, a soft smile painted on his lips and all his attention on her.

Her entire body shivered from the way he was looking at her, his need for her almost palpable. And he was an enticing sight: hair slightly mussed, jaw covered with dark stubble, and strong relaxed shoulders. He winked at her and over the din of noise, she could still hear his deep accent as he said her name, "Isabella," in that way that had become her new favorite pronunciation.

"Matteo," his mother caught his attention and gestured to the table before leaving to get him food.

His sister left her seat and as he sat down next to Isabelle, he reached out and pulled her chair so it was facing his, took her face in his hands and studied her for the briefest of moments before brushing a gentle kiss against her lips.

The entire house took a breath, deathly quiet at first, before erupting into laughter and applause. Isabelle just raised an eyebrow in question when he pulled away. He shrugged, but his exhausted excitement was almost tangible when he whispered, "Galileo."

She matched his tone, "Galileo."

He released her and pulled out a small black box from his pocket. Opening it, he gingerly held it out to Isabelle.

On a raised black cushion was a silver Moon pendant on a simple, shimmering chain.

She ran a hand over the cool surface. "It's beautiful."

"It's a reproduction of Galileo's Moon that he drew. The one Signor Conti showed us." He took it out and unclasped it, gesturing for Isabelle to lean toward him so he could put it on. "He actually helped me find this. I told him I wanted to get you something about Galileo for Christmas. I was going to get you a statue of the man. Signor Conti had a better idea." After clasping the necklace, he sat back and lightly touched the Moon. "Something to remember your Christmas in Italy."

She looked down at the pendant and placed her hand on top of Matteo's before meeting his gaze. "I don't think I'm ever gonna forget this trip."

He bent his head as their hands fell away. "Bella, would you be interested in extending your Florence stay for a few months?"

"Would I be working in a lab with a Renaissance gentleman?"

"I can talk to the university; perhaps, you can work both jobs? Come to Florence for a few days each week?"

So many ideas ran through her head – how this would look on her resume, the papers she could publish, working with Matteo.

"Yes. I have no idea what that would look like, but I don't think this is an opportunity I can pass up."

He took her hands in his and squeezed them. "Esattamente." He sat back and yawned just as his mother set a plate in front of him.

"You didn't get any sleep today, did you?" Isabelle asked.

"We set up a cot in one of the offices, I was able to get a few hours this afternoon."

Matteo's family crowded around the table as more food materialized. His sister gave a loving flick of her fingers to his head as she walked by and said, "Isabella is a treasure. Do not mess this up."

His mother tisked Sara's actions, went and kissed her son on the head, but then gave a gruff pat to his cheek as she said something, punctuating it with a pointed finger, before moving to Isabelle and gently patting her cheek.

Matteo translated, "She said she likes you and I need to be nice to you." Then he took a big fork full of the pasta that had been placed in front of him.

Sixteen people took five cars into Florence. The streets were sparse of traffic and parking. Eventually they reconvened in front of the Duomo.

After Matteo's family had entered, he stepped back, allowing Isabelle to walk first through the door and into the atrium, a transition area with another set of doors that opened to the main church.

Her feet stuttered to a stop, bumping Matteo into her. He gave a grunt, but steadied himself, moving his hands to her waist. She let her head tilt back as the darkened cathedral greeted her. The air was cool inside; no one would be taking their jackets off tonight. An echoing of soft voices and a choir that was already singing vibrated around her.

The almost cavernous space created by the hands of men was staggering. The shape of the church was common enough, representative of the shape of a cross, with a central nave and two side aisles.

Robust marble columns held the height of the cathedral in place. The floor was a maze of intricate geometric motifs done in white, black and red marble.

A sea of seats were set up in front of the high altar, but in this immense space, they were dwarfed.

She looped her arm through Matteo's and let him guide her as she craned her neck back and forth trying to take in the scene and make sense of it. Renaissance architecture, darkened stained glass windows, a painting of Dante holding his *Divine Comedy*, and larger than life marble sculptures of apostles and prophets walking out of alcoves in the walls.

Matteo guided her to the row his family had claimed, where they'd left the last two seats next to the aisle empty for them.

"It's not as full as I thought it would be," she whispered.

"It will be." Matteo shrugged. "Perhaps they are all running late."

The choir began in earnest and the entrance procession of robed priests began, walking incense and candles down the aisle, up to the altar.

The music rose to fill out Brunelleschi's awe-inspiring dome. And as Isabelle gazed up at the dramatic painting that covered the inside of the dome, she was struck by the thought that there was magic here.

Not just in this building, but in this city.

Florence had woven a web around her and she was happily, blissfully tangled up in it.

The Mass was standard, but the heady tones of the choir were illuminating, and as the final notes of the closing selection, "Silent Night," echoed and bounced through the bones of the most impressive feats of the Renaissance, Isabelle wiped tears from her eyes.

Chapter 21

Matteo's family kissed her goodbye on the steps of the grand cathedral, wishing her 'Buon Natale.' It was an unspoken matter that Matteo would drive her back to the villa. And probably wouldn't be home anytime soon.

It was twelve thirty as they walked the quiet streets of the city back to where they'd parked the car.

"This is ..." Could a person use the words magical and surreal overly much?

Matteo squeezed her hand as their footsteps echoed around them.

"Do you think we could be retracing Galileo's steps?"

"I was just thinking that. I grew up in this city, so I've always been surrounded by men of the Renaissance, but to touch one has been ..."

"Magical. Surreal," Isabelle offered.

"Esattamente."

As they drove the deserted, dark roads through the Tuscan countryside, dots of lights blinked in the distant hills. The heater did its lion's share of work as low clouds dipped and began to paint the night in shades of gray fog.

Inside the villa, Isabelle didn't say a word as she took Matteo's hand, led him to the bedroom she'd yet to use, turned on the lamp on the dresser and began to remove her jacket and shoes.

Matteo followed her lead and when he pulled his sweater over his head, she let all the pent-up passion that had built between them over the few days they'd known each other, gloriously explode.

She pulled her own sweater off as she crossed to him and splayed her hands against the naked flesh of his chest; his large warm hands slid up her sides to her back and they groaned into each other as their lips crashed together.

She had just enough wherewithal to think that kissing Matteo would always remind her of Florence and the Christmas season.

Their desperation for more became heightened sounds of heavy breathing and erratic heartbeats. A symphony in Isabelle's head.

Arms fought and twisted in their personal attempts to remove clothing and caress and run heated lips over newly revealed skin.

Matteo wrapped his hands in Isabelle's hair and pulled her back slightly so he could gaze into her eyes. His lust was evident and the culmination of butterflies and shivers and weak knees and flutters and heart palpitations that had built up over the past few days, hours, and seconds, erupted as they defined the very essence of lovers. Building to a crescendo, aching for something unseen, trying to hurry and delay the coming zenith. Matteo was possessive and heady. Isabelle, demanding and eager.

They clung to each other as they rode to new heights and their chaotic moans traveled through the whole of the villa only to dissipate somewhere in the darkness of the Italian Tuscan countryside.

Chapter 22

"Aunt Izzy, Aunt Izzy! We're here! We're here!"

Isabelle bolted upright, trying to get her bearings when she heard her name again and felt the cool air against her chest. She glanced down just in time to pull the sheet up over her nakedness as two of her nieces came rushing into the room screaming, "Aunt Izzy! We're here! Merry Christmas!"

Matteo had awoken with the sound, though it would have been difficult not to. He hadn't extracted himself from the sheets, but was trying to politely sit up.

"Who's that?"

"Aunt Izzy!" Ethan parroted his daughters as he entered the room carrying his youngest. "Merry Christmas!" He stopped when he saw the situation they'd interrupted.

"How did you get in?" Isabelle asked.

Her brother's eyes filled with a mischief she knew all too well. "It was unlocked. It would seem you were so *preoccupied* last night you forgot to lock it."

"Where's my girl?" *Oh God, her grandmother!*

"Back here!" Ethan called and Isabelle shot daggers at him.

"Did we wake her up?" Next to arrive on the scene was her grandmother and aunt.

Her brother let out a laugh. "*Oh,* we woke her up alright."

The two girls were crawling on the bed and pulling at the sheets as Isabelle gripped them around her for dear life. "Girls, maybe–"

"Who's your friend?" her grandmother asked, eyes alight with interest.

Matteo was doing his fair share of keeping the sheets in place but he nodded toward her grandmother and called "Buongiorno" to the current inhabitants of the room.

Isabelle's aunt elbowed her grandmother. "An Italian man, Mom."

Matteo started laughing when another couple joined the party. Isabelle gave him a warning look, but with a deflated sigh greeted, "Hi Mom. Hi Dad."

"Oh! Well ... goodness." Her mother's eyes widened as they shifted between Isabelle and Matteo.

"Maybe you could all give us a minute?" Isabelle asked just as everyone else pushed their way into the room.

"Would you look at that ..." Ethan's wife said.

"Do y'all mind?" Isabelle said between gritted teeth.

"I take it you weren't as lonely as we worried you would be." Ethan was really enjoying this.

"Aunt Izzy, who *is* this?" her niece demanded while giving one more tug at the sheet.

"This is not how I was planning on introducing him to you ..." Isabelle licked her lips and swatted her niece away from the sheet. "Everyone, this is my ... friend ..." her voice wavered and her sister-in-law snickered at the word choice, "Matteo."

A round of hellos and Matteo's returned grin were exchanged.

"Does he have presents for us?" her niece asked while the other increased the cringe of the moment by asking, "Was he giving you a present?"

A burst of laughter was followed by her mother's raised voice, "Okay, everyone out." She waved her hands in the direction of the door. "C'mon, let's go explore this home away from home."

Isabelle's grandmother was the last one to leave, and as she turned to close the door, she got to witness Matteo's dropped sheet, giving her a perfect view of his well-shaped torso.

"*Oh, my.* Now that's what I call a Christmas present."

"Jeez, Nana." Isabelle rolled her eyes.

"I'll guard the door. No one will bother you two." She giggled as she pulled the door shut behind her.

Isabelle hid her face in her hands for a moment, then peeked out the side at Matteo. "This is not how I wanted to introduce you to my family."

He shrugged. "It could have been worse."

"Really? How?"

He reached for her and maneuvered her under his body, his growing excitement for her evident against her leg.

She wiggled against him and pushed at his chest. "Matteo, we can't. We need to get up and get dressed."

"Your nonna is guarding the door. We have time."

She laughed and kissed him, but when it became heated she pushed him away once again; so he raised himself and grinned. "Buon Natale, Bella."

"Merry Christmas, Babbeo."

Notes to the Reader

Hi there! I hope you enjoyed the time you spent wandering the streets of Florence this holiday with Matteo and Isabelle.

-First things first. Galileo's bones are safe and sound! I promise. They are buried in the same place they were relocated March 12, 1737. But it is ture that two of his fingers are encased in glass eggs and on display at the Museo di Storia del Scienza (History of Science Museum) in Florence.

-I don't know if you noticed, but I used this year's (2024) calendar as the actual timeline for this book.

-The Casa Villa at Torre a Cona is real. That's where my entire family stayed when my sister was married. I *did* take liberties with how the actual kitchen, living room, dining room layout was like. Also, while there really is a decree that limits the hours of heating operation for all of Italy, we *never* had a heating problem when we stayed at Casa Villa. That was just for the story.

-I have never driven in Italy. I'm truly intimidated by the traffic. Of course, if I had to, I like to imagine I could.

-Christmas in Italy is more food and family-centric. There is a slower pace and no pressure to buy presents for everyone. It is more about experiences and time spent with family and friends. I love that.

-The lights that are shone on the side of the buildings aren't in the Piazza Della Signoria, but in the Piazza Repubblica. However, since I'm the writer, I get to bend the world to my fictional characters. I moved the scene because I really needed a fountain at my disposal.

-Speaking of the fountain. There is a gate around the Neptune Fountain, but again, the most wonderful thing about being a writer is the ability to just reach over and wipe out said impediments so my characters can find themselves in awkward situations.

On that note, _please_ don't swim, jump, splash or do laps in Italian fountains. And don't throw kids toys in them either. You really will be fined 450 Euros. And there truly might be repercussions where they ask you not to return to their country.

-So, here's something. The Christmas Market in Florence closes on December 18. That wasn't going to work for my storyline, so I opened it back up for Isabelle and Matteo. Just a note in case you find yourself in Florence, one of these Christmas seasons, remember to check the dates.

-A few years ago, they started a f-light festival in Florence. (I know, horrible name, but cool project.) "Various buildings in the city get lit up with video projections and special light installations ... found throughout the city. Every year the festival has a theme that connects all the different works of art." The lights are turned on December 8th when the Christmas tree in front of the Duomo is lit.

-When I write my books set in Italy, I often consult my sister who lives there. She has been insistent, from the first book, to make sure my characters are eating with the seasons. So when I asked her about popular dishes during Christmas, tortellini in broth was the answer. Of course, I did a little research and found this wonderful story:

Bacchus, Mars, and Venus stay a night at the inn. Bacchus and Mars rise early in the morning and leave Venus to rest. Rising later and thinking herself abandoned, she rings the bell frantically for the host. When he arrives, he finds the goddess in all of her splendor, naked. Struck by the sight of such beauty, in particular, the perfection of her belly button, he is inspired to imitate its glory in pasta form! He runs down to the kitchen, grabs a piece of pasta that the old maid has just rolled out, and creates the first _tortellino_...

-My friends, I wish you a very happy season, wherever you find yourself, however you celebrate.

Tanti auguri di buone feste!
(Best wishes for a Happy Holiday season!)
Cin Cin!

Acknowledgements

A lot of people kept me duct-taped together and on course while I wobbled through the editing and formatting and finally the publishing of this book.

I'd like to thank Ariane, my editor extraordinaire and A. M. Rasmussen, my amazing cover designer, who don't blink twice when I say, "I have an idea" and follow that with the information "and we don't have a lot of time to accomplish it."

Thank you Mom and Dad.

My husband and my A.

My sister Kathleen.

Amy, Gina, Jewell and Sophie. Tammy and Bryan. Lisa and Aunt Celeste.

Thank you Michele, a superb Alpha reader who catches all the little mistakes and makes me look good.

And a huge thanks to all those who shared words of love and encouragement with me this past year. I hope you know how much it means to me.

And to YOU, dear reader, thank you for your time. I know how important it is in this day and age, and I'm truly honored you choose to spend it with my words.

Want to read more by Nicole Sharp?

Try an Italian holiday

or

get started on

The **Simply** TROUBLE *Series*

About the author

Legend has it that Nicole Sharp was born to hippies during an ice storm in Stone Mountain, Georgia. While confirmation of said events cannot be agreed upon, one fact is for certain, it was a Tuesday.

By age twelve, Nicole was sure of two things: 1) She wanted to be a writer and 2) She wanted to travel. She begged her parents to allow her to voyage alone to exotic lands. They permitted her to go from California to Boise, Idaho to visit a great-grandmother.

After muddling through the college years, Nicole graduated with a Bachelors in History (think Greeks and Romans). Why didn't she major in English if she wanted to be a writer? There were better stories in history class.

Nicole is Italian. According to Ancestry.com it's a rather low percentage, but she feels that she is *at least* 51% Italian. When she returned to the homeland, she fell in love with the Italian cappuccino, so much so that she studied the language until she was fluent; thus she could order the magical elixir herself: Posso avere un cappuccino, per favore!

Nicole's first car was a yellow Chevy Celebrity and her favorite job was working as a docent in a museum in an old mining town in Colorado. She has written extensively about both.

Visit NicoleSharpWrites.com for more entertainment.

www.ingramcontent.com/pod-product-compliance
Lightning Source LLC
Chambersburg PA
CBHW031056310726
48969CB00007B/2311